Rotting De

A CIP catalogue record for this book is available from the
British Library.

ISBN-13: 978-1500751104

ISBN-10: 1500751103

1

MATT SHAW

***WARNING***

The following book contains scenes and descriptions which some people may find upsetting. Please be aware this is an extreme novel intended for a mature audience.

***

# ROTTING

# Dead

# F*CKS

MATT SHAW

Present Day

\* \* \*

There is no escape from it

## His name was Ted

No one knows where it began. Some people say it started in a laboratory whilst others say it is a new strain of the common cold which has mutated into...into whatever the Hell this is. Me? I'm not sure which category of believers I fall into. At this stage I'm not entirely sure it matters what people do and do not believe. It doesn't change what happened. It doesn't make things any better or put us any closer into finding a cure for it - if such a thing even exists. If anything - having beliefs just puts us in danger as we find ourselves tempted to get closer to the Rotting Dead Fucks in an effort to unravel the mysteries of where they came from and what they want. For all intents and purposes we should all just agree to disagree about where they came from and just go with the classic 'When Hell is full, the dead shall walk the Earth'. It's simple. It's elegant. I'm pretty sure it's a quote from the Bible too. Maybe not word for word but something similar. And if not then it is definitely a quote from a George A Romero film and - right now - those films should be our new Bible. With that question answered we can look to what they want and that isn't hard to answer; they want flesh to feast upon. I've seen these things eat brains and flesh as though they're nothing but a warm meal (like a shepherd's pie for arguments sake). Honestly they just kneel there, next to their food, and tuck in as though enjoying a dinner after a hard day's work. The noise of their teeth tearing through the flesh, the sight of the blood ejaculating across whatever surface they happen to be on,  the smell of the newly dead mixed with the Rotting Dead Fucks; a sick combination of shit, piss and death. I'm not usually squeamish but that is enough to turn my stomach.

So anyway - there you go - they're here because Hell is full and they're here because they fancy a decent meal. Problem solved. Now people can stop arguing about the silly little things and concentrate on the more important scenario of just running when you stumble into a horde. The name 'horde' was given by the news broadcasters before the power went out. The power outage; I presumed one of the R.D.Fs mistook a power cable for a person's arm and bit through the fucking thing thus causing the city-wide black out. Again, probably not accurate but what does it matter? It answers a question without the need for further discussion. Problem solved once more. Anyway the name 'horde'. I'm not sure what I think about that. See, we all have our personal preferences as to what we should call them and in this instance the news team opted for a horde of the walking dead. Usually when I turn a corner and see a massive group of them I tend to just scream something like, "Lots of Rotting Dead Fucks". I prefer that. Or even "Rotten Dead Fucks", that works too. Once I even remembered shouting something like, "Lots of fucking Rotting Dead Fucks". I found it funny when I was safely away from them but - man - that was a hell of a tongue twister. Try and say it now. Chances are, you'll stumble on some of the words at least. Anyway - 'lots of

Rotting Dead Fucks' - I like that. No one can get confused. People hear the words 'Rotting Dead Fucks' together with 'Lots' and they already know what to expect. Lots of them. It's just simpler. I digress. Where was I. Ah yes. The basics. We know where they came from and we know what they want just by settling on one god-damned answer. After that everything becomes a lot simpler; we just keep our distance. We shouldn't be getting closer. We shouldn't put ourselves anywhere near them. We should distance ourselves as far away as possible and - even then - we should continue to run. Don't look back. Don't go back for those who have fallen or been left behind. Don't put ourselves in the bite zone. Just fucking run. Just as people have varied beliefs on where these things came from, people seem to have different names for them too. Some people stick with the classics such as The Walking Dead, the Undead and even Zombies but I think those are the people who lack imagination and flare. That's why I opted for Rotting Dead Fucks. Sure the name is longer to speak out than some of the other names but - I don't know - I like it. I feel as though it has the potential to be a classic in the making. At least it would if the people I bumped into on my journeys would stay alive long enough for the name to sink in. It is always the same when I meet a new person; we exchange names, we spend an hour or so together discussing potential survival tips, we encounter a group of Rotting Dead Fucks (see, just rolls off the tongue) and - boom - they either end up getting torn from limb to limb and dead-ed or they get bitten and I have to kill them. Same end game either way; they're dead and I'm alone again. Well - nearly alone again. I can still hear it on the other side of the table I'm hiding behind. The flesh being ripped from the bone with dirty yellow teeth. At least with their lack of dental hygiene it will not be long before the teeth fall out. Like to see them try and eat us then…The Walking Gummies. I accidentally snorted as I tried to stifle a little laugh.

I can still hear the R.D.F chewing greedily so I don't think it heard me. I peered around the corner. She's still munching on my old friend, Colin. I say friend. He wasn't really my friend. If he had been - I might not have hit him in the leg with my machete. Don't judge me. I didn't have a choice. We were trapped and it was always going to be a question of him or me and - well - he's a black African and we all know those fuckers can run. He was no different; a fast fucking runner. Even with these (wannabe) Nike trainers I had looted from the store, after my leather work shoes gave up the ghost, there was no way I was going to out run him so I did what any sane person would do. I cheated.

I just did it. Didn't even think. Just swung at his leg with the rusty machete I'd found sticking out of the earth in a garden across town. Damned thing nearly cut his leg clean off. He dropped to the floor screaming, blood gushing everywhere, and I overtook him. See - I can't be that much of an asshole because I clearly remember apologising to him as I ran on by towards the door. The door. Fucking locked. And now I was here, stuck behind this little table with two doors in the room, one locked and one blocked by my fallen comrade and an R.D.F. I just hope the greedy little bastard eats all of my friend. I don't want him coming back because - man - he will

be pissed and these things are angry enough as it is. I don't
need one that has a grudge against me too. Fuck that shit.

I snuck another look around at the carnage on the other side
of the desk. The pulpy, still-twitching mess of Colin suggests
there won't be enough of him to make a grudge-fuelled
comeback. Good, One less problem to worry about. Just
leaves me and the R.D.F - some dead girl in her mid-thirties.
Going by the slit across her throat, which is allowing bits of
Colin to slip right out as she swallows down his fleshy
goodness, I'm guessing she either took her own life or was
killed by people who wanted to rob her of her possessions.
The world was always a bitch of a place to survive in but
since this has all kicked off it has become a lot worse. It is
hard to trust anyone. As Colin found out. R.I.P Colin. Know
that your death was not a waste. Shame about this R.D.F
though. She looks as though she may have been pretty when
she was alive. Her hair, now matted with blood and brains, is
shoulder length and looks as though it may have been a nice
shade of brown. Her complexion, splattered with bits of
Colin, is relatively clear (if you take away the blemishes
brought about by death). And her cloudy eyes, from the
glimpse I caught of them when I first spotted her, looked as
though they would have been a sexy shade of blue before
death's curtain closed over them. Yeah - I reckon she could
have been pretty at some point. My mind wondered as to
whether R.D.Fs could get pregnant for a split second before
focusing back to the more important task of getting out of
this room alive and unbitten.

Okay. Here's the scene. She currently has her back to me.
She is on her knees, crouched over the body of Colin. His face
is staring directly at me; a look of disappointment in his dead
eyes caused by my betrayal. Not sure why. He's in a better
place now. Lucky bastard. If he does come back to life, he
should be thanking me. No more worrying, no more stress...I
fixed upon the girl again as she leaned further forward,
raising her pert ass in the air. Her fashionably short skirt gave
me a glimpse of the pink panties hidden beneath. Weird. A
stirring from under my boxer shorts reminds me that, despite
all the death around me, I am still very much alive. Under
normal circumstances I wouldn't be surprised by my body's
reaction but right here and right now? Yeah that is strange.
Especially given the fact that said pink panties are tainted
with various stains which must have soaked into them at
time of death. Mmm. Fragrant. Jesus what's wrong with me?
Society has been down the shitter for a few days now and
already I've turned into a murderous savage. To be fair -
some might have argued I was already a murderous savage
before the events unfolded but that's not important and, for
the sake of argument, we shall simply bypass that statement.
Come on, Ted, sort it out. Right...So she is still eating. I
wonder - do these things ever get full? Do they have a
preference over whether it is dark meat or white meat in a
non-racial meaning...Although, come to think of it, even in a
racial meaning - do they have a preference? Not important.
Just another pointless debate which ends up getting people
killed (possibly by racial extremists in this instance). The door
is just the other side of her. I could possibly make a run for it.
I reckon I could get out into the corridor before she even

knew I had made a dash for it. And so what if she chases? These things aren't exactly fast on their feet. Especially this one - even in death she is sporting killer heels and one of those is broken. The only problem is - I don't know what is out there. I could be running right into a group of them. These things rarely travel alone. Hence the news readers desperation at trying to find a suitable word to describe a group of them.

Okay here is the plan. I will sneak out from where I am hidden. I will go up behind the girl, careful not to make a noise and then I'll put the blade of the machete into the back of her skull, piercing her dead brain in the process. Again - I'm not sure how these things 'die' when you cause trauma to the brain. People describe them as being brain-dead so surely it stands to reason, with the brain already being dead, harming it will have no reaction. I don't know. Whatever the science is, behind these things, fucking with the brain works so it is good enough for me. Right – enough of this internal monologue - this is it. Fight or flight? I choose fight.

Keeping low, and as silently as possible, I moved from behind the table with the machete grasped firmly in my right hand. I used my left hand as extra support, on the floor, to help keep me quiet and balanced. When I get near enough I want to jab forward with precision to ensure I pierce both skull and brain. The last thing I want to do is fall on my ass and become dessert.

The damned floor creaked under my weight as I moved ever closer to the feasting dead girl. Thank God her chewing, crunching and slurping (and even belching) is noisy or else she'd have heard me for sure. Every time a creak sounded I froze with my eyes shut tight - something about the act of closing my eyes making me feel safe for some reason; I can't see her so she can't see me. Stupid. Better served by keeping them open on the off-chance she did hear me. At least I'd be able to see her looking at me as opposed to the blackness that is my rear eyelids. I slowly opened my eyes again. She's still blissfully tucking into Colin's intestines, pulling handful upon handful out of his twitching gut. I read somewhere that if you laid a person's intestines down, in a long line, it would be about 6.5 metres in length. That's nearly a double decker bus. No wonder these things take their time when it comes to eating us. That's a whole lot of chewing right there. My mind bounced to a joke I heard once; if you laid your intestines down in a long line...you'd be dead. I never understood how that was funny. Fuck sake. Now isn't the time to be thinking about it either!

I am practically within touching distance of the girl. A nice close-up of her ass as she continues to bend over in front of me with her face practically buried in Colin's near-empty gut. The stains in the knickers both arousing me and making me want to gag. She really does fucking stink. I shuffled forward another step and raised the machete up in the air. Okay - this is it. I breathed in to ready myself to bring the blade hammering down into her dead brain.

Cough.

The scent of dirty rancid cunt and ass was over-powering. I couldn't help but cough, I told myself as I momentarily froze on the spot. She stopped eating. A second later she looked up, dead ahead. Another second and she turned to me. Her eyes filled with a burning hatred for me mixed with a wanton desire to feast upon me. I screamed as I brought the blade down hard into the top of her skull. She too made a funny noise (not quite a word, not quite a scream, just a sound) as the blade disappeared into her head with the tip re-appearing under her chin after another push down with all of my strength. Another weird noise from her as her clouded eyes rolled to the back of her head until I could see nothing but the whites. I gagged again as a thick black tar seeped from her gaping mouth and onto the floor between us. I pulled the machete from out of her skull and she slumped forward with her head in my lap. A random, disturbing twitch from below as my body decided there was a strong possibility I was about to get a blow job. What the fuck is wrong with me? I pushed the Rotting Dead Fuck away from me and onto the floor next to the body of Colin.

That takes the kill total to... Fuck, I've actually lost count. Pretty sure I've killed more of the R.D.Fs than real people though. 70% RDF and 30% human? Maybe? I'm fairly happy with those percentages. I fell back on the wooden floor, machete still in hand. I am knackered. I haven't eaten properly for as long as I can remember. Just the odd packet of crisps and bar of chocolate I tend to steal when passing shops. I could murder something proper to eat - like a great, big roast with all the trimmings...Hell, I'd even make do with a Birdseye Roast, cooked quickly in the microwave. It's too dangerous though, to light a fire and eat something cooked. I'm not sure how good the R.D.Fs sense of smell is or whether they'd be attracted to smoke caused by a fire I could light. Better safe than sorry if I want to survive this. I couldn't help but wonder whether anyone will survive this or whether this will be game over for the human population. The people now, like me, trying to forge a life for ourselves (trying to find some kind of safety) already doomed and just waiting to die without realising it. Jesus. There's a thought. For all I know Colin and I were the last two survivors. And I killed him. My mind drifted back to the sight of the R.D.Fs ass, pointing high in the air again, and I found myself thinking - if this is to be it, if I am doomed...Why not go out with a bang? I sat up and looked across to where the girl was sprawled out on the floor. It has been so long since I have felt the touch of a woman. The touch of a woman who wanted it at least. I don't count that girl I saved from the 'lots of rotting dead fucks'. Not fair to count her considering the fact I think I spent more time fighting her than I did fucking her. Ungrateful whore.

"I saved your life, don't you think you kind of owe me this?" I had asked her as I pushed her down on her knees. Little fucker had teeth alright. I remember sitting up all night, cursing her abandoned dead body, worried that I was in for the change. Thankfully she wasn't infected. Now with whatever causes the R.D.F disease at least but, I have to be honest, since that day - and our time together - it kind of burns every time I urinate. Doubt fell she passed anything to me but...Never know in this day and age.

"Fuck me!" the dead zombie girl whispered. I looked at her face. Still lifeless. I mean more so than the other R.D.Fs. Lifeless as in properly dead. Eyes still nothing but white from where they're facing the back of her skull. Did she really just talk to me again or was I hearing things? "I said fuck me, you pathetic maggot."

"You talking to me?" I asked - instantly reminding myself of the classic De Niro film 'Taxi Driver' and instantly remembering that - chances are - no one will be making another film again.

"I don't see anyone else here. Come on, fuck me. I want to feel you inside of me. I want to feel you ejaculate in me. I want to feel you empty your load. You deserve it. You came this close to death. Take me. I'm your reward."

"Well if you're sure."

"I won't fight you. Fucking put it in me."

It wasn't the first time I had heard voices in my head. And I knew they were voices in my head. I'm not completely insane after all; I know it's not the dead girl really talking and giving permission to penetrate her.

I hopped up onto my feet and crept towards the open door, still unsure what was waiting out in the corridor. I didn't look. I just quietly pulled the door shut. The good thing about the R.D.Fs is the fact most of them haven't figured out how to use a door handle yet. All too busy wanting to eat us instead of grasping the basics (which would actually make their task easier). I turned back to the recently slain dead girl, "Are you sure you want this?"

"Don't be shy. I don't bite."

"What about my friend?" I looked at the dead body of Colin. Still twitching. Still looking at me with angry eyes.

"He can watch," she said.

I'm not sure when I first started hearing voices. I'm not sure whether it was before the infestation of R.D.Fs or after. Had I always been a Sick B*stard or was it new to me? A reaction, from my brain, as I tried to cope with the world gone wrong. Not sure and now really isn't the time to overthink it. I walked back over to the two bodies and fumbled at the flies on my trousers. I'm already erect. My body knew it wanted this before my brain did - not that my brain was that far behind...I freed my penis before I reached the dead girl. I reached down to her and pulled at her legs, dragging her away from Colin. With him so close, watching, I felt weirded out. Not sure I could have maintained an erection with him there - practically breathing on us (so to speak). I opened her legs and was hit with another waft of rotten cunt. Not enough to put me off. It's a shame she is contaminated with whatever the fuck poisons them. I could sure do with a juicy taste of pussy right about now; a long time since I had tasted such goodness. I pulled her knickers down and all thoughts of licking her soon evaporated from my mind. Not surprising considering the black tar-like ooze dripping from her vagina;

16

the same stuff which pissed from her mouth when I withdrew the blade of the machete from her pretty little head.

"Just think of it as lubrication," she said. She rubbed her clitoris with one hand (in my mind) and took a hold of my penis with her other hand (again, in my mind). She didn't hesitate in guiding me in. Damn soft. Wet. Surprisingly warm despite the look of her suggesting she'd been dead for more than a few days. Fuck. They should bottle this shit and sell it via online sex shops. That is, after they've figured out how to get the Internet back online again. Priorities and all that. "How is it?" she purred.

"Fucking good." I couldn't contain my excitement as I started to build into a steady rhythm. To think, after I had killed her, I had collapsed with tiredness. Must be having my second wind. "What about you?" I asked her. "Good?"

"The best," she smiled at me with her dead face. I looked down at my cock as it pushed in and pulled out of her sopping cunt. Strings of black tar clinging to it. In my mind it wasn't black tar or anything as sick. In my mind it was her juicy cunt batter sticking to my cock. I couldn't contain myself and withdrew quickly before I moved down her body until I was mouth to pussy. My brain was screaming 'no' somewhere inside but my body (my tongue in particular) chose to ignore it and I found myself greedily lapping at her sour milk despite a gagging reflex. Don't care. So fucking horny and so...I stopped. My tongue was numb. Numb, that is, other than a strange tingling sensation as though it were trying to wake up. A burning feeling scalding the back of my throat. Eyes and nose streaming. What the fuck is this?

# Day One of the Outbreak

## Michael and Nicola

"People are advised not to..." I leaned forward and turned the radio off. My daughter Nicola was waffling away in the back of the car and I couldn't hear a word she was saying with that thing blaring from the speakers. I don't know why I ever turn it on in the first place. It's not as though they play anything decent these days; just the same old crap with the annoying radio jockey yakking over the top of it about pointless guff that I'm never interested in.

"Well can I?" Nicola asked from the back of the car. I looked at her via the rear-view mirror and tried to hide the grump I was in. It wasn't because of her. I was just never any good at early mornings despite doing them now for as long as I can remember.

"Can you what?" I asked. The 'annoyed' tone clearly audible, must try harder to disguise it from her. Not her fault, shouldn't take it out on her. I pulled up behind another seemingly endless line of traffic. What the Hell is going on with the traffic today? I'm used to it being bad but not this bad. Must be some sort of accident further up ahead. Wouldn't surprise me. The rain was beating down hard outside, so hard that I needed to drive with the lights on, and that was always a recipe for someone to crash. I turned to face her, "Can you what?" I asked her again.

"Can I stay at home today? I have a tummy ache."

Same every Monday. I am yet to get to the bottom of why she tries to tell me she has a stomach ache on a Monday morning. I've asked her what lessons she has and she always seems excited about them. I've asked her about her friends and she is always chatty about them. I've asked her about her teachers and she is nothing but complimentary. But there must be something - something which is making her want to stay away from school. Her mystery illnesses are only ever on a Monday. She never complains throughout the rest of the week. I don't know - maybe there's too much excitement for her during the weekend and it upsets her belly? I don't recall experiencing anything like that when I was younger and I'm pretty sure her mother didn't either. My mind drifted to Nicola's mother, my wife. I wish she were still with me - she'd have been able to offer some suggestions as to what causes our daughter the upset.

Vix died a couple of weeks ago now. Just before Nicola's seventh birthday. She had been ill for a while. Cervical cancer. Just came out of the blue. One minute she was fine and the next the doctor diagnosed her with that - of course it was too late by then to have much of a chance but she did her best to fight it. And I stayed with her - every minute - offering all the support that I could muster. Was never going to be enough though.

"Can I come home with you?" Nicola asked again. She was giving me the look - the puppy dog look Vix used to call it. A look I usually wasn't able to ignore. Had it been any other day I would have buckled immediately and taken her home - and that's even despite my bad mood - but today was different. My hand was forced. I had to take her to school. I had to leave her there and have some alone time. Needed to get to the bank for just after ten o'clock for a meeting with my account manager. Well - it's not really a meeting. More of a discussion about why I am behind with my mortgage repayments. More of a bollocking. Perhaps even a little threat, on their part, about taking the house back from me. Don't think like that. Need to stop that from happening at all costs. Not this home. The home I shared with Vix. Nicola's home. They won't take it away from me. Us. They won't take it away from us.

"I have some things I need to do." I told her. She didn't need to know what exactly. "But if your tummy still hurts at lunch time, I'll come and get you, okay?"

"But it is hurting now," she whined. I smiled at her as though to let her know I understood but then turned back to look out of the windscreen at the line of stationery traffic ahead of us. If this doesn't start moving soon she will miss school anyway. And I'll end up missing the appointment. Probably get home to a letter on the doormat saying the bank owns the house now!

I killed the engine, along with the thoughts of losing our house. The traffic will get moving soon enough. Just need to be patient; a virtue which is usually absent from my body until at least midday.

"Daddy!" Nicola shouted from the back. "Please just take me home!"

I took the opportunity to try and get to the bottom of her stomach bug again. I looked at her via the rear-view mirror once more, "What are you doing today?" I asked.

"I'm going home with you!" she tried her luck.

"At school. What lessons have you got this morning?" I asked. I had asked before but maybe there was something I was missing. A little detail suggesting she was nervous about something perhaps?

"English."

"And what are you learning about in English?" I asked. Maybe there was a test she was scared about. I remember getting stomach pains when I used to have to do tests, growing up. Maybe that is it.

"We're reading today. Charlie and the Chocolate Factory."

"Good book!" I said. Roald Dahl was one of my favourites growing up. To this day, I'd still happily read his work if he was alive to publish more. All children should read Dahl if only to give them an interest in reading. "What else are you doing?" She shrugged. "Honey?" She wasn't even listening to me now.

"What's that man doing?" she asked. Nicola was looking through me. I turned to her and then followed her gaze. She was staring right out of the windscreen. I turned back round

23

to see what had caught her attention. A man; walking up between the cars. His feet dragging on the slippery concrete of the road. His head nodding backwards and forwards as though his neck muscles were severely weakened. "What's wrong with him?" Nicola asked. She had noticed the blood running down the side of the stranger's face. The dazed look upon his face. Must have staggered up from wherever the accident was.

I continued to watch as people climbed out of their cars and approached the man to see if he needed any help. "I'm not sure, honey. Maybe he fell over."

Nicola changed the subject again, "Can I go home with you now then?" she asked. I didn't answer her. I kept watching the man as he got closer to our car. Someone reached out to help steady him, on his feet. The man didn't respond in the way the helper envisioned the scenario playing out. He grabbed the samaritan - hands either side of his face - and pulled him in close. The samaritan screamed out for people to help but no one reacted fast enough. The seemingly injured man leaned in close and bit the samaritan's face. People were screaming now. Even Nicola was screaming. I even screamed out. Not sure of the words which escaped my mouth but I definitely screamed out. What the fuck. The injured man ripped his face away from the samaritan who was now missing half of his own face; chunks of it hanging from the injured man's mouth. He dropped the samaritan to the floor and reached out for the next nearest person. Everything was happening so fast. People still screaming. People were running in all directions, abandoning their cars in the process. Another person screamed from near to the samaritan. I looked back over to them. Someone else was getting attacked by the injured man; pieces of flesh being ripped from their face despite their best efforts to break free from the seemingly strong monster. "Daddy, I want to go!" Nicola called out from the back.

"Okay, honey, hang on!" I ordered her. I fired up the engine of the car and drove forward into the car parked up before me. I put the car in reverse and backed up into the car behind - hitting both cars just enough to give my own vehicle some room for manoeuvring. Just enough space to spin around and head back the way we had come which was clear of traffic. Nicola was screaming despite my best efforts of offering her some reassurance, "It's okay, honey, everything will be fine."

But everything wasn't going to be fine. I'm not sure how I knew. I just knew. Suspicions confirmed when I spotted the samaritan clambering to his feet. Half of his face missing, the rest hanging off, and yet he was still getting up. What the fuck is this? What the fuck?

I yanked on the steering wheel and span the car around, bumping it up the pavement on the other side of the road. Nearly hit a damned pedestrian as they ran for cover. Had I done so, would they have got up too? I gave a final look into the rear-view mirror - at the carnage we were driving away from - and stamped my foot down on the accelerator. "Hang on, Nicola!" As soon as the car was straight we started to head back the way we came with other cars trying to manoeuvre in an effort to do the same as the mayhem continued to spread further down the line of traffic. At the speed we were traveling, ignoring the flashing of the speed camera a few corners away, it wasn't long before we were well ahead of whatever the hell was happening. Cars to the right of us slowly beginning to crawl forward thanks to the space the retreating vehicles had left behind; these poor people have no idea what was coming their way. I tried to warn them by sounding the horn repeatedly but no one seemed to care. If anything the noise I was causing only seemed to anger those who did choose to respond to me and I soon lost count of the amount of stern looks and 'wanker' signs I received for my efforts.

"Daddy, I'm scared!" Nicola whined from the backseat. She wasn't the only one. I was too - not that I could tell her so. To my daughter, I needed to be the brave one. I needed to be the one with the answers to what was going and the proof that everything was going to be okay.

"We'll be home soon enough," I told her - a reassuring look aimed at her via the rear-view mirror. She didn't look reassured. "At least you don't have to go to school today. And I don't need to go to work either. We'll just cuddle up on the sofa all day and watch cartoons," I smiled at her again. She screamed at something ahead of us so I turned my attention back to the road ahead. My heart slammed in my chest when I saw a man just standing there, in the middle of the road with his back to us. I jumped on the brakes but it was too late and the car skidded forward hitting the man, sending him up the bonnet and onto my windscreen (cracking it in the process). When the car finally stopped, the man slid off and onto the hard concrete in front of us. My heart was beating so hard and so fast I thought I was going to have a heart attack right there.  Cars continued to zoom past us by mounting the pavement. The situation not helped by the screaming of Nicola; repeating, again and again, that I had killed him. I was sure I had killed him too. Despite hitting the brakes we still hit him with some force. The horrifying thud as his body hit the bonnet; a sound I'll likely never forget.

People on the other side of the road had stopped crawling forward and were climbing out of their cars to help the man. Some of them were already on their mobile phones calling - no doubt - for help. Some of them were using their phones as camera devices instead. I threw my seat belt off and clambered from the car despite Nicola's shouting just keep driving. Wish I could but I couldn't. I need to know if I had killed the man. And - if not - I need to know if I can help him. Slowly - nervously - I walked around to the front of the car and looked down at the mangled mess of the man I'd hit. Why had he been just standing in the middle of the road? What had he been doing there? This isn't my fault. This is his fault. He shouldn't have been there.

Someone else was kneeling by his side, a man in his early forties. He had hold of the mangled man's wrist, checking for a pulse with a grave expression on his face. The words didn't need to be said but he went ahead and said them anyway, "My God...He's dead..."

I flashed a look at Nicola in the back of the car, and instantly pictured her growing up in foster care. New parents needed after her mother died and her stupid father was sent to prison for killing someone. A sickness brewed in the pit of my stomach as I imagined a time coming when Nicola wouldn't even remember my name, a time when she wouldn't care. I mouthed an apology to her but I don't think she understood what I meant.

"Has anyone called for an ambulance?" the man kneeling by the body called out to the various bystanders who were still clutching phone to ear.

A lady was first to answer, "I can't get through. No signal!" she said as she frantically hit redial.

"Same." Another man piped up as he too pressed redial on his phone. "Who are you with?" he asked the lady as he checked his network coverage on the mobile's screen.

I stumbled backwards and fell to my ass on the curb-side - close to the cars which continually drove past using the pavement as their road. Another crash was heard further down the road from the direction we had just come from. The screaming which we had been driving away from, seemingly getting closer to us as the destruction from a few streets away continued to spread our way. The man who had tried to help the one I had hit sat up like a startled meerkat – as he stared off in the direction of the screaming from down the road. I heard him ask what the hell was happening but I didn't answer him. I felt cold. Numb, almost. I had killed a man.

A loud crack came from the mangled body as its arm suddenly moved. A bone splinter popped from the elbow joint. All the bystanders jumped back in shock. I looked up too - surprised by the sudden movement. And then the man made a noise, a long drawn out sigh, followed by a groan. He wasn't dead? His arm moved again and the bone stuck out further. He should have been screaming in agony but he wasn't. He simply sat up, his neck twisted around in a direction which should have spelt out death. He slowly turned to look at me, his neck crunching with every slight bit of movement he managed. Another groan, another sigh, his eyes, oh God, his eyes, they're clouded over as though he's blinded by cataracts. Was that it? He was in the road because he was blind?

The helper rushed to his aid and instructed him, "Try not to move - help will be here soon." But help wasn't coming. Not for the people further down the road (all the screaming) and not for us. Something was wrong. Something was very wrong. I jumped to my feet and shook off the shock-induced head rush.

"Get away from him," I told the helper. I had seen this. This is exactly what had happened further down the road. This is the same thing. I know what is coming. Of course the helper ignored me just as any normal person would have done - at least, anyone who hadn't seen what we'd witnessed a few streets away. He put his hands on the man's shoulders in an effort to try and keep him still, because he was still trying to move. And then it happened. With little-to no warning the man leaned forward and bit the helper on the hand, instantly drawing blood as his teeth pierced the skin. I dashed forward and pulled the helper away from the supposedly dead man. He was screaming and holding his fresh wound. The people who'd been trying to make calls on their phones were already running back to their cars whilst the ones who'd been trying to take pictures were now taking videos instead. "Get away from him!" I called out to anyone close enough to hear me. I told the bitten helper to get back to his own car as I hurried back to my own car - careful to run around the broken body of the man to save from also getting bitten as it continued to try and stand up, another crack of bone. I jumped into my car and accelerated over the mangled body. A bump-bump noise from under my wheels as the car's suspension did all it could to adsorb the impact. As we drove on down the road I couldn't help but look in the rear-view mirror at the scene we were leaving behind. The man I'd hit with my car twice was still trying to move and now it appeared the helper was also attacking someone. What the fuck is this? Nicola was crying in the back of the car as we joined other cars in speeding away from the scene. She was watching out of the back window too. No hiding this from her then. "Hold on, honey, we'll be home soon!" I told her. Not that I'm sure what good being at home was going to do. The way this thing was spreading - whatever it was - it was rapid. This is bad, this is bad...I kept thinking over and over again.

## The First Reports

All the television channels had come away from their scheduled programs to report on what was happening across the country, the country- whatever it was, it wasn't just local. It was countrywide. All of the newsreaders read from the auto-cue with serious tones in their voices. Their expressions were even more serious. All of them were saying the same thing; infected people were attacking anyone and anything. A few of the newsreaders were replaced, on the screen, by various amateur videos from across the country showing the devastation and showing more examples of infected people attacking normal people.

CCTV footage from the port showed people running from a boat - some cruise liner usually associated with luxurious travel to exotic islands for the rich and well to do. Another angle showed bodies, some twitching, on the top deck of the same liner. Cut away to an airport and people were seen running from that too. Through the glass-paned front of the building it was possible to make out more of the infected attacking vast groups of people who, seconds later, seemed to get up and also join in with the violence. It didn't seem to matter who the uninfected were - whether they be children, elderly, disabled...They were all fair game and open to attack. Over the footage of the airports and ports - the newsreader advised against travelling to those destinations saying there was no way out to be found there. Sensible to mention it really considering the amount of people who'd have the first thought to just jump on a plane, or boat, and try and leave the country. The footage on screen changed to that of a shaky hand-held camera nature, perhaps taken on a small camcorder or someone's mobile phone. The footage showed someone being bitten by one of the Infected before someone else came along and pulled them away - a scene very much like the one I had watched at the time of my accident when I had tried to help the man who was attacked. This time, though, the man who pulled the man away was also attacked and bitten. The camera didn't stop filming though. It stayed focused on the man who was bitten first. He was flailing his arms and legs around. He was seemingly screaming out. An agonised expression on his face; twisted and tormented as though he was desperately trying to fight the infection killing his body as it surged through his bloodstream. And then the man went still - Deadly still - Stood bolt-upright. A second or two later and he moved again - jarred movements. His mouth biting at nothing as though he hoped something would just present itself to be bitten. His eyes cloudy, just as the eyes of the man I'd hit had been. On camera he turned and looked right at us. The camera dropped to the floor and the screen cracked but we could still see enough to know that the newly bitten man was lurching towards where the camera man had been. I'm guessing from the way the camera was dropped - he wasn't there anymore. No doubt running away as fast as his legs could carry him and I don't blame him. The television cut back to the news reader back in the comfort - and safety - of his studio as they continued to keep us informed as to what was happening and warn us that - if bitten - we risk the infection too. It is not airborne, the reports said, but it is carried in the blood. It is carried in the saliva. Contamination means certain infection.

I felt a coldness run through me as my mind couldn't help but think about all of the horror films I had watched, as a youth, seemingly coming true. Across all the channels the same story but, from flicking between them in an effort to find answers, none of them seemed to give answers as to why and how. More importantly - none of them seemed to say where we should go or what we should do. Most just suggesting to us, for the meantime, to lock our front doors and wait for help to arrive. Not to travel unless we absolutely have to. I turned the television off when Nicola came into the room from her nap. Poor thing had more or less crashed as soon as we got in through the front door. Thankfully - whatever it was spreading out there - it was quiet back at the house, quiet in our little close too. Some of the neighbours cars were missing from their driveways and others were still parked up as though they'd been abandoned, just as I had abandoned my own car on the front lawn, as close to the front door as I could get without actually driving through it. The houses which looked occupied all had their curtains shut as though blocking out the horrors in the real world and shutting the occupants into their own private sanctuary. I wasn't sure if that would help, if it meant extra protection, but I figured I'd do the same and - when Nicola went off to lie down as I suggested - I went around the house closing the curtains too.

I gave her a smile, in an effort to hide my fear and show her everything was okay, and asked, "How's the tummy?" She didn't come over to where I was sitting in the living room. She just stood there, in the doorway. "Did you hear me?" I asked.

"Why's mummy standing in the garden?"

## Dr. Platt

I was sitting opposite my eleven o'clock appointment with a neutral expression on my face, listening to the wild fantasies he had about raping and killing people and all I could think about was the fact I would make a good poker player. I'm disgusted with my patient. I'm almost scared of him (hence the reason I need to have Darron Hayes sit in, on the appointments, with me). Yet he has no idea what I think about him. He just thinks I am here to listen to his (mildly amusing, at times) rants and issue his prescriptions when he tells me he is running low. I can see Darron in my peripheral vision, sitting to the side (and slightly behind) my patient. Just as well really because he hasn't quite mastered the same poker face that I have spent years mastering. I couldn't help but wonder whether this was actually a poker face I had learned or whether I had just become used to the horrors that I hear in this small box room; my office.

"And how did that make you feel?" I asked when my patient stopped ranting about his latest escapades. A standard question used in order to get more insight into the patient's mindset. His name was Ted. Ted had been coming to see me for about three months now, originally referred to me via his G.P who was concerned about Ted's anger issues and general behaviour. Ted was a strange case. He had gone to his doctor to discuss his unbalanced anger issues because they were of concern to him but - on all the times I've seen him - he has seemed proud of his temperament. It's almost as though he isn't here to get 'fixed' as he initially put it, on our first meeting, but rather to brag and sound off about his violent fantasies. I had taken his case to the board, as we do with all new patients, and advised them of my own feelings (being that I was uncomfortable to have him on the streets as he posed a possible threat to others or himself) but they had overturned my suggestion of a possible stay in one of our care facilities - where we could get to know him a little better without outside influence. Apparently it was because that - although he openly spoke about his violent feelings - he had yet to act upon them. He had never been in trouble with the law, he had never acted out his fantasies and he was being cooperative with regards to help offered (in the form of therapy and medications).

We were getting to the end of our hour together and had barely achieved anything that I had wanted to; another session wasted listening to how he likes to follow pretty, young girls whilst playing rape scenarios out in his head. And they don't think he is a danger to anyone. Who are they kidding? In my professional opinion - it is only a matter of time before he takes his first steps into acting upon his wants.

"I wanted to fuck her!" he told me. He was talking about a young girl he'd followed home from the shops. He had gone into great detail about what she was wearing; a short skirt which barely covered her buttocks, a white shirt which was almost see-through and high-heels which accentuated the length of her legs.

"Did you talk to her?" I asked him. I already knew the answer. He never spoke to the girls he supposedly followed. Part of me wonders whether he even followed the girls in the first place, or even saw them. A little niggling doubt that he's simply making it all up just to have something of (supposed) interest to say. He shook his head. Of course he didn't talk to her. He never does. Either he saw the girl and didn't say anything or he is making the whole thing up and his imagination isn't quick enough to make up a story about what he said to her. Either way I was getting tired of him. In truth, I was getting tired of all of my patients. I had been doing this for far too long now. Coming up to twenty five years this coming February and it's the same thing day in and day out. I rarely get to help anyone, as I originally believed I could when I first started all those years ago. More or less, I end up tending just to be a sounding board. A sounding board who can keep people, like Ted heavily medicated.

"Just remember walking around, you know, with the biggest erection as I thought about what I wanted to do to her. As I thought, you know, about how tight her cunt would be. And wet." He licked his lips and I had to hide the shiver which ran down my back. He was a scrawny man in his late twenties not attractive but not ugly - just plain, largely let down by his inability to properly groom himself. It was the same routine every time he left the appointment, I'd end up having to spend five minutes spraying the room with air freshener and opening the windows to try and air the place before the next patient came in. The joys of a small room and the necessity to keep the doors closed during my consultations; it really seals in the stink. "I ended up going into a clothes shop," he said, "just grabbed any old shit from the sides and dashed into the changing rooms. Whacked one off right there and then." I shifted in my seat as my mind kept screaming at me to just have him sectioned - but it wasn't that easy. I couldn't just do it myself. I always needed others to sign off on it and, contrary to what people think, the process isn't that straight forward. "Fucking shot my load all over the mirror with some pretty girl just on the other side of the curtain, waiting for me to finish. She knew what I was doing. I could tell by the smile on her face when I left. She wanted me." The guy is delusional. "Probably licked that spunk right off the mirror," he laughed.

"Listen we're coming up to the end of the appointment but I think I'd like to try you on some new medication," I suggested. I didn't wait for him to confirm whether he was happy to try something new before I started writing out a new prescription on the pad next to my keyboard. "And then I think it would be a good idea to see you again in a week to see how you're getting on." We usually had two weeks between sessions but the way he was speaking to me seemed to be getting worse - his fantasies getting more explicit with each appointment. A week would give me enough time to talk to one of my colleagues again, perhaps let them meet him too. See what they think; whether the man is lying about his escapades or whether there is a possibility of him actually doing the acts he is speaking about.

If it's the latter than we have a duty to get him off the street whilst we try and help him. We have a responsibility to the safety of the general public.

I finished scribbling the notes - on the prescription pad - and tore the top sheet off before handing it to him. He took it with his dirty hand. Filth trapped under the finger nails. He stood up and extended his hand towards me.

"Until next week then," he said. I smiled and stood with him before shaking his hand. Sweaty. It's because of this I have disinfectant in the top drawer of my desk.

"Yes. If you need to reschedule, please do not hesitate to call in," I told him. He turned and walked from the room, closing the door again behind him.

"You get all the colourful characters, don't you?" Darron said. He wasn't laughing. If anything he appeared to look sorry for me. He clearly doesn't envy my position. I just raised my eyebrows as I reached for the air freshener (in the top drawer next to the disinfectant). I started to spray the room and Darron took the moment to leave the room, "I'll make sure my diary is free for next week," he informed me. I guess it would have been prudent to check that he was free before making the extra appointment with Ted but - worst case scenario - I can always get someone else to sit in on the session. Perhaps, even, my colleague.

Darron closed the door as I reached across the desk to open the windows. Instantly I was hit by a sound I wasn't expecting; the sounds of screaming and distant alarms singing through the mid-morning haze. I leaned across the desk in an effort to try and see what was happening but - considering the level of noise - the road outside seemed eerily deserted. I'm not entirely sure why - perhaps a little spooked - but I slammed the window shut and left the office. There was shouting coming from the waiting area at the end of the short corridor between office and reception and I immediately recognised two of the voices; Darron and Ted. I hurried into the room to find out why they were arguing. They were standing by the front door which was being blocked by the receptionist (not that she could have stopped anyone from leaving).

"What's going on?" I asked. They ignored me as they continued to shout at each other. The receptionist was saying it wasn't safe to leave, Ted shouting that we had no right to keep him here and Darron doing his best to keep the peace. There were other patients, and staff members, in the room too. They were keeping themselves to themselves and all looked uncomfortable with the situation.

"Let me the fuck out!" Ted screamed again. He went to push the receptionist but was blocked by Darron (who was considerably bigger than Ted, which helped). "You can't keep me here!"

"It's not safe out there!" the receptionist yelled again.

"You're all insane!" Ted argued. "It's you lot who should be having therapy, now get out of my way."

"Will someone please tell me what the hell is going on?" I shouted.

The receptionist looked to me, "It's gone crazy out there...Reports all over the news that people are attacking each other. They're talking about some kind of infection."

"What?" Ted was right, the receptionist (Tina) was the one who sounded as though she needed the therapy.

"On the television," Tina continued, "I was watching the news on my break...In the staffroom...They're attacking each other."

"Where? Who?"

"Everyone and everywhere. It's gone crazy out there! We can't leave here! It isn't safe!" She was pale and shaking. I turned to one of the nurses who was standing in the doorway and asked her to fetch Tina a cup of tea with lots of sugar (to help with the shock) and she kindly obliged. I then turned back to Tina.

"What are they saying exactly?"

"There's been an infection outbreak...."

"From where?"

"They didn't say. They said that it is bringing the dead back to life..."

I turned to some of the other staff members who were in the waiting area, "Has anyone else seen this?" One of them, a young girl, stepped forward and nodded. "People are attacking each other?" I don't know why I was finding it so hard to process the information in my mind - I had heard the screaming when I opened the window so I knew something was wrong. And the deserted street. Fair enough it can get quiet from time to time but the road outside that window is rarely completely empty. In fact, I don't think there has ever been a time when I haven't seen at least one person walking down it or at least one car driving out there. I looked at Tina who was visibly shaking. With no warning she went to pass out only to be caught by Darron, who had to let go of Ted. He helped her across to a chair, in the corner of the room, and instructed her to take it easy a moment. Ted took the opportunity to run from the building, slamming the door behind him. I hurried over to the door and quickly locked it. I'm not sure what was happening out there or what people think they have seen but - given the reaction of the people in this room - there is little point in taking any chances.

"Okay no one else leaves then, not until we know what is going on," I said. Not sure why I'm suddenly in charge but seeing as no one else is keen to step forward - I'm as good a person as any. "We all stay in this room for now. All stay together."

Darron piped up, "I'll go through and bring the television in," he suggested.

"Fine." He left the room and headed for the staffroom. A man on a mission. I turned back to Tina. She was sweating now and looked as though she were hyperventilating. Her reaction is what scared me more than anything else. Normally a quiet woman, she had seen a lot working the front desk of this establishment, so for something to scare her it had to be serious. I approached her, "How you doing?" I asked as I crouched down next to her.

"My dad is at home, do you think the carer is still with him?" she said. Her voice was meek. Her father was elderly and needed a lot of care; something she arranged for him a few days of the week to enable her to leave the house and try and live a little.

"I'm sure he is fine," I tried to reassure her. "Why don't you use the phone and give him a call?"

"I tried but I couldn't get through." She started to cry. I didn't know what to say to make her feel better. Funny, really, considering my line of work. I gave her shoulder a squeeze of reassurance and stood to my full height. "I'm going to go and see where your drink is," I told her. I hurried from the room before anyone else asked me what we should be doing, or sought reassurance from me. I needed to know what was going on. I needed to see what she'd seen - what had spooked her so. I walked down the corridor and took a left turn into the staffroom. Darron was sitting there, on one of the chairs, leaning forward with his eyes transfixed on the television set. A genuine look of concern on his face. I was hoping he would find some hope in what he saw on the news. I was hoping Tina had just over-reacted but - judging from his face - it was far worse than I had imagined. "What is it?" I asked. He didn't answer. He tried to, he just couldn't find the words. I looked at the television screen and baulked at what I saw; absolute pandemonium. I pulled up a chair and sat down next to Darron. "What could have caused this?" I asked him. He didn't answer me. The way he was fixed upon the screen, I wasn't even sure that he had heard me.

The program we were watching seemed to be on a continuous loop. Watching the whole thing, until it looped back to the start of the report, it was about ten minutes in length and offered no real answers. Just terror at a world gone crazy. Infected people biting other people and infecting them in turn; no word of what the actual infection was or what caused it. The main point of the television report being to tell us to get indoors, secure ourselves there and await help or further instructions. The whole thing was bleak. It's no wonder Darron couldn't take his eyes from the screen or that Tina worried for the safety of her elderly father. I leaned forward and turned the television off when it was clear we had seen all that it had to offer.

"We don't need everyone to see that," I told Darron, "unplug it." It would only cause them more panic if anyone else was to watch the footage and that wouldn't help the situation. The only message they needed, from the news report, was that we needed to stay indoors and wait for help (or further instructions).

"What do we tell them?" Darron asked.

"Other than needing to stay indoors? Nothing. We tell them nothing. If they press for information - maybe tell them there

is a situation occurring but the reports didn't really go into
it." I sighed, "I just think it will make everything worse if they
see any of that. They'll panic and when people panic - things
go wrong." Darron nodded. I hadn't explained myself as
eloquently as I could have done but I still got the point across
and that was all that mattered. We both stood up and Darron
lead the way back to the reception area where everyone was
patiently waiting for answers as to what was going on.

"Where's the television?" one of the patients asked.

"Couldn't move it but Tina was right - something is
happening outside but it's not saying what. It just says we
need to sit tight and wait further instructions." Darron
responded "I'll check on it in a bit," he said before someone
asked how we were to await further instructions if no one
was there to monitor it.

"So what do we do now?" someone else asked.

"Now we close the blinds and we try and be as quiet as we
can!" I said. If things are really as bad out there - as the
television seems to make out - then we don't want those
things trying to come in here. We need to be as quiet as we
can. Especially given the fact I heard screaming, at the open
window of my office, suggesting those things are close by.

Darron pulled me to one side, "What about your patient?"

He was referring to Ted. I shrugged. It may not have been
professional of me but what was I supposed to do? Suggest
we send out a search party? The man wanted to leave. We

couldn't force him to stay here, even if we wanted to. He was a free man and it was his decision to make. As far as I was concerned, he was gone and we were better off for it. When the world wasn't broken, I wasn't comfortable with Ted being out there amongst it. Now the world is damaged, I'm fine with him mingling with its inhabitants.

Darron continued, "We're not going to try and get him back?"

"No."

I think my answer shocked Darron. He knew me as a person who wanted to help others - especially those who appeared helpless. Until now, he had never seen me turn my back on anyone but things had obviously changed; both out there and inside of me. Now it was all about survival. I approached the windows and let the blinds down - further proof that I wasn't prepared to put us at risk for the benefit of someone such as Ted.

## The Security Office

Anyone watching the CCTV monitors in the morning wouldn't have seen anything out of the norm; people were coming and going. Maybe venturing out to their places or work, maybe heading off on school runs, or possibly even going to the shops before the stores got busy. There was certainly nothing to raise any levels of concern. When things did change it seemed to happen, in various parts of the city, at the same time; it was almost impossible to determine where the starting point was. It was certainly too much of a challenge for the one person - who usually sat in the room monitoring the situation - to keep track of.

Now - heading into later morning - all of the monitors showed the same thing; complete carnage and mayhem. There was a camera down the road from the school which showed a number of infected children - and a handful of teachers - lurching their way from the school gates. Some of them just standing there as though there was nowhere for them to go. Some of them feeding upon what used to be one of their classmates or colleagues. The monitor next to that screen, on the same shelf, showed a few streets away and the situation wasn't that much better; a couple of people running down the road - apparently screaming not that the monitors had any sound outputs - and some of the infected people milling around in front gardens as though they had changed, suddenly, whilst doing their daily chores.

Closed circuit security cameras at the airport and dockyards showed more of the same, which had already been shown on the news channels only with less survivors and more of the infected.

The monitors which showed the pictures captured by the cameras for the main shopping street (Market Street) showed it to be practically empty. Just one person standing there. It was hard to make out who they were because of the distance they were standing away from the camera but it wasn't hard to see what they were doing; standing there, outside of a shop, casually tossing what appeared to be a rock up into the air before catching it again.

The picture on screen zoomed in - controlled by the nervous operator - in an effort to see what the person was doing. The first thing the controller noticed was that the man was smiling. The first smile witnessed on the cameras since the start of this infection. Smiling? The security officer leaned forward, unsure whether she was really seeing this? Someone smiling and seemingly at ease at what was happening? The officer shifted uneasily in her seat. What kind of person enjoys days like these? She didn't have an answer but she knew this was the reason why she was staying put, in this office, with the door shut. And - with that - she witnessed the man throw the rock through the window. The man threw his arms in the air, as though enjoying his moment of triumph. Seconds later he dove through the hole left by the shattered glass.

The security guard went to phone through to the police, as part of her job, but stopped short from picking the handset up. She knew this was just the beginning and she knew the police were too busy dealing with the infected to care about the odd looter.

Ted

I like the sound of the broken glass under my feet. My heart is still racing from smashing the window. The feeling of power. The feeling of being able to do what I want without anyone telling me it is wrong. I'm not sure what is happening, I'm not sure why the streets are deserted, I'm not sure what the hell is going on but I don't care. This is my time now, bitches. This is Teddy Time! Okay, that seemed a little gay but that's not a problem. I have time to work on it.

I cast my eyes around the shop - a small newsagent - and immediately spotted what I was looking for; the drinks fridge. Something about pouring my heart out, to that fucking shrink, just makes me thirsty. You'd think she would offer me a drink, or something, but - no - never so much as a cup of water. Just rude. If I see her again, if shit gets fixed, I'll talk to her about that. Make sure I at least get a cup of tea, or something.

A noise from the back of the store pulled my mind back to the game at hand. The store sign said it was 'closed'. There shouldn't be anyone in here.

"Hello?" No one answered me. Something back there, moved again. Someone is definitely there. "Who's there?" I asked. Something fell off a shelf and smashed on the floor. Yep.

Someone is definitely back there. "I was walking past," I lied, "and your window just fucking shattered...I don't know what is going on out here but shit has gone crazy what with quiet roads and exploding windows which most definitely haven't been smashed with rocks..." I hesitated. Another thud. "Okay it was me but if you come out, I'll pay for the damage. I was just really thirsty and needed a drink and your door was shut and there was no way in and...what the fuck?" A Muslim shop assistant staggered into the doorway, just behind the counter at the back of the shop. "Are you okay? You're bleeding." She had blood running down the side of her head. Did my rock somehow ricochet off a wall and twat her back there? Is that even possible? To be honest, not entirely sure why I give a fuck even if that was the cause (however unlikely). She looked at me. A weird look on her face. One, if I am going to be honest, I didn't recognise. "What is it?" I asked. She was groaning, trying to say something, as she continued to lurch forward. She passed by the counter until she was standing on the shop floor with me. She looked angry. Angrier than anyone I had ever seen before and that is saying something considering some of the people I'd seen sitting in my doctor's waiting room. "Okay," I told her, "that's close enough." She ignored me, kept lurching forward with that look in her crazed eyes. Boy - did I pick the wrong store to break in to. "Did you hear me? Stop coming for me," I ordered her, "I won't be able to be held accountable for my actions." As she continued to near me, I got my first whiff of her. She fucking stinks. What is that? Some kind of fucking spice? Why the fuck can't they eat normal food? Our country, our menu! I moved to the next aisle across to give me a little more distance between us. For two reasons, to get away from the smell and to also get away from her as a person. The madness in her eyes was making me feel uncomfortable. She muttered something else as she continued to approach at the slow, unsteady pace. The more I hear her talk, the more I'm sure she is speaking shit in her language. No wonder it sounds like fucking gibberish to me. I felt my blood start to boil - not just because she was ignoring me but because I realised she was refusing to go along with the English way whilst trying to make a living in our country. "Look, love, you want to fit in around here - you need to make the effort. You know what I mean?" Only some racking was between us now. I grabbed the closest thing to hand which happened to be a can of beans. Not the best of weapons, if I am going to be honest, but if need be I'm sure I can do some damage with it. She groaned again. Probably calling me a cunt, or something equally demeaning. "Look - you come closer and we're going to have problems. I've apologised for the window, like a gentleman, and I've been polite to you - all things considered but, you keep coming for me, I'm going to bash your fucking brains in. Understand?" She groaned again. Was that a 'yes' or another one of their words for 'cunt'? If there is CCTV in here, people reviewing it will see I gave her plenty of fair warning. I lobbed the can of beans at her head. With just the racking between us, it was practically point blank. The tin bounced off her head with a satisfying thud before it hit the floor and rolled under the racking which separated us. She groaned again and took a swipe at me, over the racking, with claw-like fingers. "Jesus, woman, take a fucking hint already." I grabbed another can from the racking. Big Soup. No warning this time, as she continued to try and claw my face, as I pelted her full force in the face. The force jarred her head back with a satisfying crack. By the time she lowered her head back to looking forward again, she had fresh blood streaming from her nose. More groans. Must have broken the nose for sure. The blood looks practically black in this light. Immediately she went back to trying to claw me again. "What is fucking wrong with you, you psycho?" I have to admit, I was impressed with her high tolerance for pain. No doubt she'd been hardened by being raised in a culture which likes to whip and stone their people. Coming over to this country, my fucking country, must be like visiting Disneyland to these people. I grabbed another can from the shelf (spaghetti) and caught sight of something across the other side of the shop - something which would have been much more effective. A wooden baseball bat hanging next to other toys (footballs, frisbees and other cheap tat which really has no place in a store like this). I grabbed another can from the shelf in front of me and - again - smacked the woman in the face. Harder this time. She groaned but, other than that, barely registered the hit. Okay. Fine. Let's see how she gets on with a baseball bat to the face.

I made a dash down the aisle. By the time I reached the end the fucking woman was already lurching her way down to intercept me. Have to be quicker than that, though, as I darted across to the other side of the shop. She hadn't even made it all the way to the end of her own aisle before I had a hold of one of the baseball bats. I ripped the packaging, which secured it to the hook, from the handle and held the bat up high. "Only wanted a fucking drink!" I reminded her as she continued to close in on me. She groaned again and I answered her with a swing of the bat. The bat connected to the side of her head with a satisfying thwack noise and she crumpled like a piece of paper. Still groaning though. What the fuck was she saying to me? I was startled when she started to get back up again - a fucking blow like that, to me, and I'm pretty sure I wouldn't have gotten back up. "I just want a fucking drink! What - seventy pence at most? You really want to fucking die over a drink?" I lifted the bat again over the top of her head. So easily I could just bring it down onto her and end the stupid whore's life and it's pretty tempting to do so. Not as though she deserves to be in our country, using our resources...Doesn't even speak my fucking language what with her grunts and groans. I put the bat against her forehead and pushed her back to the floor, pinning her there for a moment, and even then she kept trying to reach up and grab me with her waving arms. The woman is a fucking soldier! I kicked her in the stomach and hopped over her body - back towards the fridge which had originally got my attention when I first walked into the shop. "Because you've been a dick," I called back to the woman, "I'm going to take a couple of drinks. And a bar of Snickers. You only have yourself to blame!" I opened the fridge with my spare hand and took a couple of cans from the fridge. I shoved them in my coat pockets and slammed the fridge shut again before walking across to the chocolate counter. As per my promise to the stubborn bitch in charge, I grabbed a Snickers bar. I tucked the bat under my arm and opened the sweetie wrapper with my left hand and my teeth as the woman continued to crawl over to me. Jesus. Let it go already woman. It's open now. Can't exactly sell it now can you? Just put it down on your wastage log and - boom - you're good to go. As I took my first bite, I felt the woman tugging at the leg of my jeans. I looked down at her. To think - I was happy to let her live but...Clearly she wants to push me. I put the chocolate bar in my mouth and clamped it there between my teeth. I turned towards the woman. I raised the bat in the air. A second of hesitation - a chance for her to change her mind - and then I brought it crashing down on the back of her skull. Her groaning stopped. "I was going to let you live, you stupid cunt." I shook my head as I took a hold of the chocolate bar and helped myself to another bite. "I was going to let you live." I swallowed. "Oh - and, just so you know, I'm taking the bat too."

I turned my back on the twitching corpse of the stubborn bitch and walked towards the exit of the shop. I say the exit. It's not the proper exit. It's the one I had made with the help of my trusty rock. As I stepped out into the cloudy mid-morning day I couldn't help but to think today has been a good day. Funny really considering I usually have terrible days when I am forced to go to my psychiatrist appointment. I stepped away from the broken glass and looked up into the sky. I closed my eyes and breathed in deeply. Today is definitely a good day. My moment of joy was short-lived as I heard the sound of another Muslim fuck. What? Really? I opened my eyes and looked across the street. Another one of them was heading across the pedestrianised area of the road, right towards where I was standing. Really? Must have heard the commotion and come over to investigate; groaning the same shit she had been groaning, same look of hatred in his eyes. Fuck, if they hate us that much - why are they even in the fucking country? Go home! Not rocket science. Go home to your own country and you won't have to put up with us robbing you, killing you or just generally irritating you. You'd be happier. We'd be happier. Win, win for all!

"Just fuck off!" I yelled at him. "I only wanted a drink. They were shut. Every fucking shop is shut! What was I supposed to do?" The man answered me with a what sounded like another fucking groan. "I don't understand what you're fucking saying, you prick! We're in England! Speak English, motherfucker!" I held the bat up as he continued to approach, "What you want some of this too? Do yourself a favour and turn around!" Another groan to the side of me caused me to spin on the spot. Yet another Muslim headed my way. Say what you want about these fuckers, they have a strong sense of community. To think, growing up, I didn't even know my next door neighbour's name. To me he was just some old fart living alone in his house who occasionally banged on the wall because I was being too loud.

"Quick! Over here!" a voice called from one of the shops further down the road. I looked over, as did the Muslims, to the person shouting out. Finally. A white person. I didn't know them but they were waving directly at me. "This way! Quick!" they shouted again.

"You're fucking lucky!" I pointed the bat at the Muslim closest to me before lowering it and running in the direction of the person calling for me. In truth it was me who was probably lucky. Pretty sure, after these fucks saw what I did to their friend (probably mother, sister or daughter in fairness) in the shop, they'd probably lynch me as part of their own sharia law. Not sure I'd even make it in front of a judge to explain that I had only wanted a Coke.

As I neared the middle-aged man, he held the door to his shop open (another fucking newsagents) and ushered me inside. No sooner had I stepped foot into his property did he slam the door shut and lock it.

"Quick!" he said, "Help me block it with something." He positioned himself next to some racking, which ran down the centre of the store in sections, and pointed for me to grab the other end - which I did (temporarily pinning my baseball bat under my arm). Together, and spilling most of the crap off the shelf in the process, we moved the first section of racking until it blocked the door. "That'll hold them but we can't stay in here. More will come. They always do. This way!" he didn't wait for me to say anything before he was already headed down to the other end of the shop and a small door with a 'staff only' sign attached to it. Again, like a gentleman, he held the door open for me. "Through here." I couldn't help but think of the difference between the way he was dealing with me and the way the Muslim woman tried to handle me. Had I come to this shop first, the man would have probably just given me a Coke without me even needing to ask for one. Clearly the woman was a racist. The man pointed to some stairs, "Up there!" I did as instructed and ventured up the stairs. There was another door, at the top of the stairs, which was shut. The man rather rudely, all things considered, pushed past me and opened the door. He went through and I followed.

"This is where you live?" I asked him. He closed the door behind me and locked it using the actual door lock and a security chain. "You really think they'll be that pissed?" I asked. "All this because I was thirsty...Jesus Christ." The man looked at me with a perplexed expression on his face.

"What are you talking about?"

"I broke the window, I admit that, and I may have been wrong to do so but all of the shops - yours included - were shut and I was thirsty. Just wanted a Coke but the woman, she kept coming for me so I had to defend myself. Next thing I know I have, I guess, her entire family out for my blood."

"What exactly do you think is going on out there?"

"Sharia Law I'm guessing."

The man frowned at me. A split second later he was laughing. "You think they're like that because they're Muslim? Are you really that stupid and ignorant?"

"I'm going to let that slide because you helped me out of a tricky spot but if you talk to me like that again..." I looked at my baseball bat and then at the man before giving him a smile. Sometimes words weren't needed.

"You've been wandering around out there and the only thing you notice is the colour of someone's skin? You haven't noticed anything else that other people - normal people for instance - may find slightly fucking odd?" I didn't like the way he was talking to me. What started off as a potentially great friendship was starting to take a downward turn for the worse. "Come with me," he walked me through to the lounge and pointed towards the television which quietly played in the corner of the room. "You might want to take a seat," he suggested, pointing to one of the two armchairs in the room.

Michael and Nicola

Nicola looked towards the patio doors on the far wall of the lounge. I had drawn the curtains blocking out the outside world so she couldn't see anything out of them (and nothing could see in) but it didn't stop her from trying.

"Why's mummy standing in the garden?" she asked. I jumped up with my back to the glass doors.

"Mummy's not here," I told her, "you know that. She's in Heaven."

"No, she's not."

"Yes, she is." I felt myself getting angry with Nicola. We had spoken about what had happened to her mummy at great length, so she could understand. I even had specialists help explain it - to try and minimise the emotional damage at losing her mother at such a young age. I tried to calm myself down. With everything that has happened today the chances are she's just had a bad dream. A horrible nightmare brought on from the day's drama.

"No, she's not! She's standing in the garden!" Nicola yelled at the top of her voice. I nearly lost control, right there and then. Nearly slapped her in the face but managed to pull myself back from completely losing control. The shock of the day, the anger at the way Nicola spoke to me and the hurt at losing Vix - it's all too much for me. "Look!" before I could stop her Nicola stormed across the living room floor to the curtains and gave them a sharp yank open. I froze. My heart in the back of my throat. There she was, my wife, standing at the back of the garden with her back to us. I knew I couldn't see her face from where I was standing but I knew it was her just from the dress she was wearing. I had spent so long, going through her various outfits, trying to find something to bury her in. Such a hard decision. I'd never forget the dress I ended up choosing. Figure hugging, light blue, pretty - nice shoes which matched it perfectly and the undertakers matched a haircut she had in one of my favourite photographs. She didn't look quite as good as the day I buried her though. Something was amiss. Her hair was disheveled, the dress hung from her as though too big from severe weight loss and she was coated, head to foot, in a dusting of earth. But - inconsistencies aside in how she looked now to how she looked the day I had her buried - she was still my wife; the love of my life.

For a split second, Vix hadn't died. For a split second my life (Nicola's life) was normal. For a split second, I was happy. We were happy. Nicola was already fumbling at the key to the door in order to let her mum come home. It was the sound of the lock clicking open which snapped me back to the harsh reality; the truth of the matter. This person - this thing - standing in the garden, it wasn't the wife that I had buried.

There was nothing about my wife inside this monster. Just a passing resemblance.

"Mummy!" she called out as she opened the door.

"No!" I quickly pushed the door shut before Nicola could get out. I ignored her screams as I turned to look out of the glass doors. The thing - the monster - standing at the back of the garden, started to turn around slowly. "That's not mummy!" I said. I quickly shut the curtains before Nicola saw the thing's distorted face. That on top of everything else she saw today - if there is a way out from the horrors - she'll never recover. In fairness, if I saw the new face of my wife, I probably wouldn't have been able to forget it either. I picked Nicola up and took her to the other side of the room. She was still screaming so I put my hand (gently) over her mouth to try and keep her quiet. "Honey, listen, I know you think it is mummy but I promise it's not. It's not her!" She stopped screaming so I slowly pulled my hand away.

"But it is!"

"Oh, darling, it's not her. I wish it were..." I wanted to give my daughter a hug. I wanted to show her that I wasn't being a bad person. I was protecting her. Now wasn't the time, though. A fact reiterated when a hand banged against the glass patio door. One bang, and a second. A third. Repeatedly banging to try and get in. Nicola screamed with each bang of the pane. "Listen we have to leave. Go and get your shoes on," I told her, "as quickly as you can for daddy, okay?" She turned on the spot and ran from the living room, down the hallway, towards where she had kicked her shoes off when we came in. I hadn't taken mine off. I rarely did when I came home (something which pissed my wife off, especially if she had spent the morning hoovering). My wife (not my wife) was still banging on the outside of the glass patio door. I turned around and looked at the closed curtains covering the patio door. They were shaking slightly, from the force of my wife banging on the glass. I wanted to go up to them, and move them back. I wanted to see her. I wanted to see if I could see any trace of her in there but I knew I couldn't. It wasn't my wife no matter how much I wanted it to be. Whatever is happening, whatever is bringing people back to life, it's not because they want to rekindle old romances and continue with their lives. There is nothing innocent about what is going on. They're coming back bad and that is it. I turned away and left the living room, joining my daughter in the hallway.

"Ready?" I asked her.

She nodded. The poor girl looked terrified.

"Where are we going?" she asked.

I didn't know. The news programs showed the port and airport both out of action and told people to stay locked in their homes until help showed up but I don't think anyone on the news was expecting things to be as big as they were. I mean - my dead wife climbed from her grave and came home. I'm pretty sure, if she did it, other previously buried corpses will be doing the same thing. And if not now then soon. Nicola was looking at me, those damned puppy dog eyes, expecting an answer. No ignoring the question this time around. I thought on my feet, "Off to see Nanny and Granddad!" I told her. Vix's mum and dad lived out in the country - a big, old house right slap bang in the middle of nowhere. I already knew the roads close to us would be a nightmare to negotiate but, if we could, there was a good chance we would be safer with them, away from the dense population of the city. The news of a visit to Nanny and Granddad brought a smile to Nicola's face. Pretty sure this was the first time I'd seen her smile today. "Sound like a plan?" I asked. She nodded. "Good."

"Wait, I need my bear!" and before I could say anything she dashed up the stairs towards her bedroom. Her teddy bear, Ivor, she hated to part with him. The banging hands of my wife, bouncing off the glass door in the living room, reminded me that we didn't really have time for this but if it meant Nicola felt more comfortable then we'd have to find the time.

"Hurry!" I called up. I hurried over to the front door. Down the side of the door there were a small section of glass windows which you could look out of (or look in through, I guess). I used them to peer out into the street. Shit. A few of the infected milling around out there. Thankfully - so far - none of them seem to be that close to our house, or my car, but I'm well aware that could change any minute. I turned to Nicola as she came bounding down the stairs. "Got it?" I asked - a rhetorical question seeing as I could see the little brown bear clutched in her dainty hand. She joined me at the bottom of the stairs. "Okay we're going to play a game," I told her, "we're going to go outside now and we're going to see which of us can be the quietest on the way to the car. If you make a noise, you're out!" I was relying on her love of off-the-cuff games to get us to the car without attracting any unwanted attention. "The winner gets to eat the last of the Haribo sweets stashed in the glove box!" I promised her. If her love of off-the-cuff games doesn't keep her as quiet as possible then her love of sweets will, I'm sure. "Okay?"

"Okay!"

I gave her a smile and made my way back to the front door. I pulled the keys from my pocket, where I had slipped them when we came in, and checked out of the small glass window again. Still the same out there - a few of those things lurching around but not a lot else happening. I wondered whether any of my neighbours were out there, in their houses, waiting to do the same as Nicola and I. Maybe it would have been a good idea to wait to see if they made it first before I put my daughter in danger. Can't. The banging on the glass reminded me that time was of the essence. I opened the door as quietly as I could. Thankfully no creaking hinges to bring unwanted attention. A quick check to my left and right - to be sure the coast was clear - and I ushered Nicola out with a gentle shove of my hand. Other fathers may have wanted to lead the way but I'd rather she went out front so I could keep a better eye on her and anything (or anyone) that may have been approaching. Harder to be mindful of her if she were behind me, whilst also trying to ensure I didn't run into trouble too. Thankfully - abandoning the car where I had - it wasn't that far to go and we were soon both inside via the same door. Nicola crawled on through to the back seat and I made myself comfortable (quickly) in the driver's seat. The car door, even though I closed it quietly, gained the attention of a few of the infected but they weren't close enough (yet) to cause any significant issues. I slid the key into the slot and twisted it. The engine spun into life and immediately all of the nearby creatures knew we were there. Slowly they started meandering towards us - all of them looking as though they were struggling to control their bodies. I could sense Nicola starting to panic but there was no need. Not whilst we were in the car. With half a tank of petrol and the doors locked - as long as we didn't park up in the middle of a group of these things - we were pretty safe for now.

I slid the gear-stick from neutral to 'one' and gently pressed my foot down on the accelerator. No need to rag the engine yet. Not whilst we weren't in any imminent danger. As I drove away from my house (possibly for good) I couldn't help but think of my wife (at least what was left of her) standing there trying to get in through the back door. Part of me wished I'd had the energy and heart to put her out of her misery. Let her rest in peace as she deserved to. I can't beat myself up about it too much. I'm not sure how strong these things are but I know what happens if one of them manages to bite you. I couldn't afford to put myself in any danger. Not whilst I have a daughter to look after. She is my priority. I don't give a damn about myself - I haven't since the passing of Vix - but Nicola...I don't want her to suffer or be in any pain. I want her to live her life to the full and I'll do anything I can to ensure that is the case.

I started to think about her Nan and Granddad and couldn't help but wonder whether their house was indeed the sanctuary I believed it to be, not that I have much of a choice now my own home had been compromised. And I still think the middle of nowhere is a good a place as any to try and wait this thing out. At least there, surrounded by fields, we have a chance of setting up some kind of watch to ensure these things don't get close to the house. The more my mind weighed up various options, the more I felt this was definitely the best of decisions. As I turned onto the main road and saw all the cars queuing to get out (mostly abandoned) and with so many people running around it was hard to tell the normal people apart from the infected I knew my biggest challenge would be in getting to the property.

"Daddy I'm scared!" Nicola whined from the back of the car. I knew there was no way of stopping her from seeing what was happening; the panic, the attacks, the desolation. That didn't stop me from wishing I could keep her from seeing it though. I didn't admit it to her, for she didn't need to hear the words, but I was scared too. Very scared.

I double checked that the doors were locked before pressing forward with our journey trying my best to navigate my way through the abandoned vehicles, panicked pedestrians and infected souls feasting on whomever they could grab. Sadly, and as expected, it wasn't long before Nicola and I attracted unwanted attention. Not by the infected who were happily eating those already killed but by some of the remaining survivors who were banging on the windows, and trying our locks, in an effort to hitch a lift with us.

"Daddy!" Nicola screamed as a man (clearly bitten on his neck) banged on the window next to her.

"It's okay, honey. Everything is fine. Just ignore them. We'll be out of here soon..." Driving around the cars, mounting the pavement where necessary, and zigzagging across the road it wouldn't be long before we were out but I knew that this was nothing to what we were going to witness. This was merely an appetiser. I reached down and turned the radio on. I wasn't sure what to expect but part of me hoped they'd still be issuing some kind of travel bulletin. Some kind of information about the state of the roads and which of the routes was most congested.

"People are advised not to travel. Stay in your homes until help comes."

"And when do they think help would come?"

It didn't take long to realize that the talk show host was talking to some government bod. I turned the volume up as I continued to navigate my way through the varied vehicles and bodies.

"We are doing everything we can to try and ensure this situation is resolved swiftly," was the only answer the host received. We had all seen this situation arise in horror films and other works of fiction but I couldn't help but wonder whether there was actually a real contingency for this kind of scenario. Maybe there was or maybe the people who were in charge of that area just brushed it under the carpet saying it could never happen. For the sake of humanity, I hoped it wasn't the second case.

"And what exactly caused this?" the host pushed for more answers. I already knew he wouldn't get anything. Even if the man he was talking to knew - it would be so classified he wouldn't be permitted to say anything for fear of sparking more panic.

"We are still following up some leads," the man clearly lied. They didn't have a clue as to where it came from. Someone - somewhere - must know but it certainly wasn't the people in charge. I could sense the man sitting there now, in front of the guest slot's microphone, squirming in his chair. The fact he was there may not have been answering many (any) questions but at least they had gone to the effort of getting someone there. Being able to hear a voice with no answers was better than hearing no voice at all.

"So once again people are reminded to stay in their homes until help arrives. Do not travel anywhere. The ports are full of the infected, as are the airports - with all planes grounded. Lock your doors, close the curtains and remain as quiet as you can. We are being promised that help will be...." the radio cut off mid-sentence. I leaned forward and twisted the dial off and back on again but it was completely dead. Maybe it will come back on again in a minute, or two. Probably just a technical glitch or something...Try it again when the roads are a little clearer - when I have more time to have a fiddle. In the meantime, things are getting even more congested and I need to concentrate. Just keep driving for as long as I can - and then, when I can go no further, turn back to the nearest safe place to hide for the night before starting again tomorrow. I know it will be slow progress but so long as it is progress that will be fine by me.

## Dr. Platts

I walked back through to the staffroom where Darron had gone to listen to the news. I had grown concerned after the lights switched off in the main reception area. Trying the switches in the other rooms, on the way through to the staffroom, revealed it to be more than a blown bulb. All of the power was out. Darron jumped when I entered the room. It probably didn't help that this room had no windows at all so was pretty dark already - despite it only being midday.

"Scared the hell out of me," he said. He didn't get up from the chair he was sitting on.

"Sorry." I nodded towards the television, "Did they say anything else?"

"No. They just keep playing the same thing over and over again on loop - as they were doing before." He gestured towards the waiting room with a tilt of his head, "How are the people doing?"

"They're scared," I told him. There was no sense trying to sugarcoat it. No one knew what was happening and all of them felt afraid. They were scared of what was going to happen to them. They were scared of what was happening to their loved ones. They were just scared.

"How about you?" Darron asked. A genuine look of concern on his face. I wasn't sure whether he was expecting me to lie. Perhaps - he thought - if I said I was okay, it would give him some hope too? "How are you doing?" he pressed.

"I'm a little apprehensive," I didn't lie. "We have no food, no electricity and no idea what is going on out there. We're being told we need to stay here yet we do not have the provisions to do so. This help that they say is coming - how long do we give them before we have to move on?" I could tell by Darron's expression that my words brought him no comfort whatsoever. If anything he looked more worried than before. He had opened a floodgate though and I couldn't stop, "And if we do leave - where are we supposed to all assemble? They're telling us the ports and airports are closed. Clearly major cities will be rife with infection and danger. That doesn't really leave us a lot of options. Never mind the fact that any kind of travel will be dangerous." I stopped a couple of seconds to catch my breath. I expected Darron to speak but he said nothing. We both knew there was nothing he could say. All the points I raised were valid and of genuine concern. Realising he wasn't going to fill in the silence, I continued, "If we stay here tonight - will that make it safer to venture out in the morning or increase the chances of running into the infected?"

"I don't know."

"The longer we leave it, the more chance there is of the infection spreading to more people - you know it and I know it."

Another silence fell between the two of us. Darron was the first to break it, "So what do you suggest?" he asked. "What should we do?"

"It's not up to me. People should be able to make up their own minds but I think we should leave. Sooner rather than later - whilst there is still some daylight."

"You don't think it would be safer to travel at night?"

"I don't know. I don't know anything. You asked me what I thought and I'm telling you," I could feel myself getting angry. Not because of Darron questioning me but because - for once - I felt as though I had no control whatsoever. In my career I had always tried my best to help people (not always succeeding admittedly) but I had never felt out of control. This was new territory to me and I didn't like it. Not one bit.

Darron went along with my line of thinking, "I suppose there is more chance of stumbling into trouble in the dark," he reasoned. Not entirely unreasonable to think that. "At least in the daylight we can see them coming and do something about it." He hesitated, "We just need some idea of where we can go."

"Maybe we could put it to a vote?" I didn't feel comfortable making the decision for everyone else. No one had the right to make such choices. I noticed Darron was looking at me as though he wanted to say something but wasn't sure how to bring it up. "What is it?" I asked him outright.

"What's what?" he looked away from me. I didn't say anything. I didn't feel the need to remind him that I was trained to read the body language of people - some of whom being desperate to try and hide what they were thinking from me for fear of the repercussions. Darron breathed out heavily and I knew - there and then - I wasn't going to be impressed with what was going to come from his mouth. "I just think that maybe..." he hesitated, "....look we don't know what is waiting for us out there. Do we really want to go out with a large group?" For once I found myself lost for words. I just looked at him blankly. Darron was staring at me, clearly waiting for an answer. An answer I didn't have. Was he really suggesting we just abandoned the people here? He was a care-worker, just as I was and yet here he was ready to drop his principles at the first sign of trouble. Surely, we of all people, had a duty of care for the people with us? "You know we have a better chance of survival - out there - if it were just the two of us."

"Have you heard of the saying safety in numbers?" I asked him.

He didn't answer immediately. He looked as though he was weighing up his potential answers. Probably contemplating the one which painted him in the more positive of lights.

"If we go out there," he said after what must have been a couple of minutes, "with a group of scared individuals - some of whom, let us not forget, aren't of the most stable mind...We will be drawing attention to ourselves. If we go out, just the two of us, then we have a good chance of getting somewhere where we can safely wait this out...Whatever it is."

"Well you seem to have some answers so where do you think we should go?" I asked. I wasn't agreeing to anything he was suggesting, I just wanted to see what else he was thinking. Maybe at least one of his ideas may have been feasible. He didn't say anything. Just shrugged. "Look - we'll stay here tonight. We shouldn't leave the building without any idea of where to go. We'll just be running around out there like headless chickens - whether that's in a group or not." He didn't disagree with me about this at least. "And I suggest you keep your thoughts to yourself," I continued, "we don't need them panicking that we're thinking about leaving them behind."

"But you agree with me it's the best thing to do?" Darron carried on trying to push me. I didn't think it was the best thing to do. I think we should all leave together. I think we should stick together. We could (and can) all look out for each other. And I honestly believe that. "Well?"

"We just need to lay low for the night and sleep on it. See how we feel in the morning. The most important thing - for now - is to try and think of where we can go. We need to think of the most secure place where we can wait for the help they're talking about."

"And what if there is no help?"

I sat in one of the armchairs next to where Darron was still perched. The thought had already crossed my mind that there wouldn't be any form of help - but I hadn't yet admitted to myself the scale of the possibility. From what I had seen on the news - earlier - this thing had taken hold of the city fast. Even if there was a way to get survivors out, I'm almost positive it won't be something they'll be able to implement with any haste. Darron didn't need to know what I was thinking. With the way his mind was working, he was already struggling to hold it together and think rationally. "Help has to come. They're probably already on their way round the city. I'm sure it's just a matter of time," I knew I was rambling. I shut up before I said anything stupid.

"If we need to spend the night considering what are the best and possible outcomes for this - we need to consider the fact that no one is coming for us. We need to think about going it alone."

"You're going out there alone?"

Both Darron and I turned to the doorway. Tina was standing there. She might not have heard all of the conversation but she certainly caught enough of it.

# Day Two of the Outbreak

## The Security Office

The power had been out for a few hours now with no signs of restarting. The security office had a back-up generator, which allowed for a little light during the otherwise dark night but this didn't impact the monitors which had been entertaining (and horrifying) the security officer with their captured moments. She shifted forward in her seat and hit the closest monitor she could reach as though it would magically bring it back to life. Needless to say it didn't and the screen remained as dead as half of the city's population.

Had the monitors been on the security officer wouldn't have enjoyed her evening's viewing. She was hoping that, by watching them religiously, she could see help start to sweep through the city (no doubt in the form of the military) or evidence that humanity was winning the battle against whatever was trying to extinguish it but that's not what the monitors would have shown. This first night of the mysterious outbreak reaching through the city (and, unbeknownst to many, further afield) showed no signs of hope. If anything it showed something far worse; humanity losing the fight and more innocent people falling foul of the infection as it continued to spread beyond any possible control.

One on one it wasn't hard to fight off an Infected person so long as you avoided getting bitten and - had the cameras been filming - the security officer would have seen people fighting them off on numerous occasions but, as the numbers of the dead increased, she'd have also witnessed the tables beginning to turn. As soon as there were more than one of the infected to contend with - things became a lot harder, if not impossible to escape without getting (at least) bitten.

Throughout the streets during the night, people were getting bitten as they made their way for provisions or someplace which they thought to be a 'sanctuary' from the madness. Some of the people 'turned' and some of them went on to get torn, literally, from limb to limb - all depending on how many of the Infected were attacking them. One 'bites', more than one 'shreds'.

The picture on screen wouldn't have been much better from the camera pointing to where the looter was hiding either. That street - the one with the shops - seemed to be attracting a vast amount of infected. All of them seemingly congregating outside of a single newsagent. All of them clawing at the glass, desperate for what was hiding within.

Ted

As the sun slowly rose into the sky robbing us of the peaceful darkness (admittedly littered with dangers), a thought struck me. A new name for these assholes. Sure I had heard what the news people had called them before the power went out but that seemed pretty dull. And clearly - going by my new friend's reaction - Muslim Fucks wasn't acceptable or accurate.

"I've thought of a new name for these things." I was looking out of the living room window of Harold's small flat above his shop. Harold being the man who had called me into the building before I got my ass chomped by the Muslim fucks outside. The Muslim Fucks themselves were crowding around outside the shop window we had earlier barricaded. I had been watching them all night. What had started as a small group gradually increased over the hours until there were many more and just as I thought that was it more would lurch their way up the street; all groaning and stinking. Not all of them were Muslim though. Now the group was mixed. Still all of them stunk. "Rotting Dead Fucks!" I continued my original (insightful) train of thought. Harold didn't answer me so I turned away from the window to look at him; make sure I had his full undivided attention. He was just staring at me. Guess he wanted me to explain -

something I'm only too happy to do considering we have fuck all else in common to speak of. "You see...I got it because they're rotten, right, they're dead and they are most definitely a bunch of fucks." I paused. I won't lie. I kind of expected a 'well done' or something similar. I thought it was insightful. Not just that, actually, I thought it was fucking genius. "What? Nothing for that?"

"You need to come away from the window." He had been telling me that all night. Like a broken record going round and round and round. After the first half hour of 'you need to come away from the window' I had got a headache. How I hadn't pummelled his head in with my trusty baseball bat I'll never know. "We should have left when we had the chance," he continued, "how many out there now?" I shrugged. "Roughly?" he pressed me for an answer. I could stand here and count them if I wanted to but what was the point? Exact numbers - at this stage - meant nothing to us.

"Lots of rotting dead fucks," was an easier answer and one which needed no further explanation. "Don't you have a back door we could use?"

"Yes but there's no way of seeing out of it without it being open. If there are lots of....them...."

"Rotting Dead Fucks..."

"Quite. If there are lots of them out back then we won't be able to keep them out once the door is open." He paused a moment. "The news was saying we should stay inside. Maybe we should. We have food downstairs."

I looked out of the front window again, "As well as a fuck load of rotting dead fucks," I reminded him. He was right about the food situation we had here and - so far - they weren't getting in but would the window last? The more that kept showing up, pressing on the window, the more chance they'd come through it. I looked at my new friend and felt a pang of guilt - a new feeling for me. Had he not come out and helped me then he'd probably still be locked away in here - but without a shit load of R.D.Fs banging on his storefront. "I'm sorry," I said to him. Another first for me. Apologising to someone. It felt weird.

"For what?" he asked. He looked at me. He looked tired. Hardly surprising considering he hadn't slept all night but then neither had I. Mind was too busy thinking of all the shit happening outside.

"If you hadn't opened the door for me, I'd probably be pretty dead by now." Watching the way these things seem to come together, out there, it's a fair assumption. It's easy to take one down but a group of them? Probably not as simple. "And you probably wouldn't have been surrounded by the cunts." I paused a moment to reflect, "Probably both be in a better place." I surprised myself again as I realised what I was doing; bonding with another person. I couldn't remember the last time I had done that.

"Nothing to say they wouldn't have found me by now. Besides what kind of person would I be if I left you to become one of them?" He got up from his settee and stretched his back. "I'm going to get something to eat from downstairs. If you want - you're more than welcome to take what you fancy but try and stay out of sight of the window. Probably wouldn't be a wise thing to try and antagonise the infected." I didn't correct him when he called them the infected although I wanted to. It was his place and I was a guest so, I guess, he gets to call them whatever he wants to. Just shows a lack of imagination on his part. He disappeared out of the flat and down the stairs towards the shop. I hesitated for a moment as another - more troubling - thought popped into my mind; if he shows lack of imagination with how he speaks of the R.D.Fs then surely that means he doesn't have the imagination to come up with a plan to help get us out of trouble. A thought followed by an imaginary scenario popping into my mind; a scenario which saw us in trouble and Harold doing nothing to help me. I tried to shake it from my mind but I couldn't. Was I really wasting my time shacking up with someone who had the potential to get me killed because they couldn't think their way out of the proverbial box? Maybe I'd just be better off getting out of here and going it alone. Haven't had many friends before this point, I don't see why that should change just because the world has gone to shit.

I walked over to the doorway and stood there, at the top of the stairs, listening for Harold. I could hear him downstairs as he tried to sneak his way around the shop without being spotted by the R.D.Fs. Credit where it is due, he's being pretty quiet. My mind was still split in two; I could go downstairs and help him grab whatever we fancied to eat or...The back door of the shop was at the bottom of the stairs

- easy to just leave. I quietly crept down the stairs until I was at the bottom where I froze. As quiet as I was trying to be, there was no stopping the bastard steps from creaking under my feet and I wasn't sure whether he'd heard me. I listened. All I can hear is him scavenging and the sounds of the R.D.Fs at the window. I peered around to see if I could see him and I could. Look at him, in there, sliding around the tiled floor of his shop on his hands and knees - a carrier bag hooked around his wrist filled with what looked to be sausage rolls and other pastry items taken from the fridges. Guess he has to eat them now before they spoil. He hadn't spotted me. I turned back to the back door and placed my ear against it. It's made from heavy metal - no doubt to stop people from trying to break in. Hard to hear anything on the other side. But maybe that's because there is nothing to hear? I put my hand on the handle and my other hand on the key sticking from the lock. The lock 'clicked' when I gave the key a slow twist. Was kind of hoping that it would have been quieter by going slower. No such luck. I stood there, a moment, still unsure of what the best course of action would be.

"What the fuck are you doing?" Harold's voice from behind me. Close. He must have been in the doorway to the shop, just a few steps behind me. Panic clearly in his voice. Can't say I blame him - I'm not feeling too great about this situation myself.

"I can't stay here," I said, "it's a bad move."

"A bad move? It's our only move. We don't know what is on the other side of that door."

"But we know what's on the other side of the other door and they don't look as though they're giving up anytime soon. It's only a matter of time before they come in and you want us to sit upstairs and wait? You ever watch horror films? I do. I watch a lot. My psychiatrist believes I should stop. She says they do nothing but fuel my dark thoughts but that's bullshit. I just like 'em…."

"Please get away from the door…"

"You see, in horror films, whenever the victim knows there is an intruder in the house - they always run up the stairs. Needless to say we all know they're going to die within the next few minutes when the killer - or killers - discover them hiding in a closet. They usually die gruesomely too. Well that's you and me if we stay here."

"You're not talking any sense. We do not know what is out there. For all we know the whole building could be surrounded by the infected. For all you know you're about to open the door right into a group of them and - once you do that - there's no turning back for either of us. You hear me?"

"Now picture the same film…The victim finds out there is a killer in the house and so they run out of the back door. They don't stop running. They're like Forrest Fucking Gump, you know? Just running and running until, before they know it, they're safe and sound in another town completely. The killer meanwhile is still searching the house wondering what the hell went wrong…You know why we don't see people leave via the back door?"

"Please just lock it back up and come away…"

"Answer the fucking question. Play the game."

"Please…."

I felt the rage build within me again. Harold and I would have never been good housemates. I know that for sure now. We were too different. I was smart and savvy and he was just - well…He opened a shop in what appears to be a Muslim community. That isn't smart. They won't shop with him when their own kind is right next door. And I have to be honest, the other store did seem to have more stock on the shelves. A little of this and a little of that. Something for everyone. This store seems flat in comparison. I asked him again, "Why don't we see the victim run out of the back?"

"I don't know….Why?"

"Because there's nothing out there to make the film interesting. Nothing but safety, and people who watch horror films - they don't want to see that shit. They want to see the person get butchered. Just the way it is." And with that I pushed the handle down and kicked the door open with my left foot.

## Dr. Platts

We were all standing in the reception area still with the
blinds shut. The room was a little lighter so we knew the sun
had come up behind the closed blinds. Tempers were frayed
- just as they had been for most of the night after Tina
reported back to the rest of the group what she had heard
Darron and I discussing. Of course I had tried to diffuse the
situation by telling them it was nothing more than a
discussion and that no decisions had been made. I hadn't
gone into whose idea it had been to leave the group because
I didn't think it would have been fair to Darron but that
didn't matter because Tina had heard everything and filled
the group in on the details I had purposefully omitted.
Needless to say the group had taken it quite badly with a lot
of hostility aimed at Darron - some name calling, a little
shoving from one of the male patients who was trapped in
here with us. It was only by reminding people that - if we
continued to shout at each other - there was a good chance
we'd attract whatever was out there waiting for us. It
seemed to do the trick and the group went quiet.

Regardless I didn't sleep a wink. I don't think anyone did. I
could just sense everyone watching each other as though
waiting for someone to make a move (no move in particular,
just a move in general). We hadn't even been in here for

twenty-four hours and yet already the group was rotting with distrust and fear.

Darron walked over to the window and carefully peered out through the edge of the blind, being as careful as he could not to make it apparent anyone was in here. I didn't say anything to let him know I was awake and watching him. The way he was moving, quietly, I could tell he thought most of us were still asleep.

"Trying to sneak off?" a voice called out from the back of the room. I didn't roll over, from where I was lying, to see who had said it. I didn't need to. His name was John Hankins - one of my more troubled patients (and the man who was supposed to be following Ted's appointment yesterday). I had seen John for a little over a year now and, of course, tried him on various medications. He'd suffered abuse at the hands of his father when he was younger, and had spent a lifetime going into and out of different correctional facilities since he was fourteen years old. Most of the time it was petty crime he'd be caught for but I knew he was capable of much, much more and I knew - one day - he'd likely just snap. The way he was talking (and looking) at Darron yesterday, I thought that day had come. With that in mind, though, he'd never so much as raised his voice at me directly. He'd only ever been polite and respectful of me. Strange to know you're in the presence of a monster and yet not fear for your safety. Yet, with Ted, I knew he hadn't done anything but I feared every alone moment with him.

Darron stepped away from the blinds, "I was trying to see if I could see anything out there," he said. His tone carried a certain amount of hostility towards John - clearly the two men were still at odds from the events of the previous night.

"And?" I jumped in before they started again.

"It looks clear. I can't see anyone."

The road was a frequently used pathway to get to the shops but - other than this building - there wasn't a lot of reasons for people to be milling around outside so Darron's declaration didn't come as a surprise to me. There were no schools nearby and no major shopping areas. There were just houses and by the time everything apparently kicked off yesterday - most of those would have been empty as the occupants would have ventured off to wherever they went for their days.

"Well you'd better fuck off then!" John piped up again. I sat up and looked across the room at him. He was sitting in the receptionist's chair - his eyes fixed on Darron with a look of hate brewing in them. I wasn't sure whether this all stemmed from last night's conversations or whether there was something deeper rooted between the two of them of which I was unaware.

I looked over at Darron. I could see, in his face, that he desperately wanted to tell John to do the same thing. It was good that he didn't. Both men were fairly big and - given the circumstances - I'm pretty sure it wouldn't have taken much for either one of them to step the hostility up a notch or two.

Despite Darron ignoring John's comment, John continued. It was clear he just wanted to get a rise out of him, perhaps even antagonise Darron into making the first move. That way, if John put him down, he could claim it was self-defence without losing the respect of any other members who were trapped here. "Go on. You wanted to go it alone so now's your chance. There's nothing out there. You said so yourself so...Fuck off." He pointed towards the door. "Don't worry - we'll make sure to close the door when you're out there by yourself."

Darron bit his lip. "We were just talking options through," he said after a moment taken to reflect upon what he was going to say. "I didn't know what I was saying. I apologise. I was just talking out loud. This is a pretty bad situation and I didn't know how best to deal with it. Yes, for a moment, I thought it may have been better to go it alone. It may have been...But my mind wasn't made up and I..."

"It didn't sound like that to me," said Tina. I closed my eyes in disbelief that she'd felt the need to get involved. She knew John Hankins too. She'd seen him, once, kick off in the waiting area over the slightest of things (such an insignificant matter that I can't even remember what it was about). The fact she'd seen the extent of his temper though meant she should have known better. "You wanted to leave with Veronica," she said, "just the two of you. Leave the rest of us here because we'd slow you down..."

Darron looked across the room to me. I could tell by his expression that he wanted me to back him up but I couldn't.

Tina knew what she'd heard and - if we were going to go with that story - we needed to have done it last night when the arguing first started. If we changed the story now people would know we were lying. "Veronica," he urged me to speak.

"What are you still standing there for?" John verbally pushed him. "There's the fucking door. Use it." John stood up. Thankfully he didn't step out from behind the reception desk so there still wasn't a clear path between the two of them.

"Back off," Darron spat, "I told you - we were just talking last night and nothing was decided...Just airing some thoughts..."

"Don't give a fuck what you were doing last night," John continued, "the group has made their mind up and we don't want you here. So - whether you want to go it alone or not - the decision isn't in your hands anymore. I say again - there's the door. Fuck off out of it."

"Oh? The group has decided that have they?" Darron turned to everyone else in the room and looked from face to face. I watched their reactions too. Most people looked away, avoiding his eye contact. There were eleven people in here, including Darron and I, and it seemed as though no one was willing to speak out in his defense. They were all weak individuals of mixed ages - the youngest being a seventeen year old girl called Amy and the eldest being a woman, with depression, who looked to be in her sixties. "Veronica?" he looked at me again in a hope I'd speak up for him. I couldn't not.

"Last night - tempers are high. People are scared," I said.

"Of course they are," Tina hissed, "it's hardly surprising, is it? He thinks we're going to slow him down out there so he wants to just leave us here to die. Why would people not be scared?" I could tell - at this point - arguing wasn't going to solve anything.

"That's not how it was," Darron continued to try and back track from his story. He looked flustered. John stepped out from behind the desk and I felt my heart rate increase a notch. He approached Darron and put his hand on his arm before pulling him towards the door. Darron tried to break free, "Get your fucking hand off me!"

"Look we all need to calm down and talk about this in a civilised manner," I protested.

"You two had your talk last night. He wants to fuck off and go it alone so I'm helping him!" John grabbed Darron again and shoved him towards the door. Darron reacted by swinging for John as soon as he caught his balance. The punch connected hard but John seemed to barely register it.

"Darron!" I knew it was too late now. It didn't matter what anyone said. Everyone backed away from the two men - myself included - and watched in horror as they squared up to each other. "This isn't helping!" I shouted but I knew neither of them could hear me through their own internal rage. John responded to Darron's punch with a hit of his own which sent Darron back against the glass door. He hit it so hard I thought he was going to go through the damned thing.

"Please just stop." Darron darted forward, head down, and threw his body against John's - the force was enough to send the two men over the reception desk and onto the floor behind, out of sight. The contents of the desk slammed to the floor around them. John was the first to stand up. He wasted no time in putting his foot into what was likely to be Darron's stomach; I couldn't see from this angle.

"Get up you cunt!" He raised his hands as though ready for round two.

Darron's bloodied hand stuck up from behind the desk. It slammed down onto the wooden top and pushed down as Darron pulled himself to his feet. The room gasped. Even I did. A pair of large scissors sticking out from his chest. Panic written all over his face as he looked down at the handle. He looked up at me with teary eyes, "Veronica..."

I went to cross the room towards him so I could help but was held back by Tina. There was a crazed look on her face, "No!"

"What are you doing?" I asked, "Let go of me!" She wasn't even looking at me. She was looking at the two men. I followed her gaze. John was staring at her. He nodded as though the two of them were having a private conversation. I wasn't the only one to scream when John leaned forward and ripped the scissors from Darron's chest before repeatedly stabbing him with them. Darron's body buckled under the shock of the penetrations but was stopped from falling by John holding him up with his other hand. I cried out for him to stop but I knew my words weren't heard (or were ignored) and that it was too late anyway. John released

Darron long enough to change his hand position on his body. He grabbed Darron by his hair and leaned in close to his face - as though he was getting a kick out of watching the man die. Again I begged for him to stop, just as some of the meeker members of the group were doing the same, but he didn't listen. He took the scissors and, without so much as blinking, stuck them in through Darron's eye socket. He let go of both Darron's hair and the scissors and the two dropped to the floor, lifeless. I too dropped to my knees coughing and hacking and, seconds later, vomited onto the floor. Tina - this usually quiet woman - was laughing behind me. "You're a stupid bitch!" I hissed at her as soon as I was able to form the words.

"I'm sorry - what was that?" she asked. There was a tone in her voice that I'd never heard before. As though she believed she was the one in charge. The silly woman had no idea, though, that there was only one person in charge now and he was standing next to the corpse of our mutual work colleague with blood on his hands. We could have all got out of here together. Darron would have come to his senses and we could have all survived this. Together. Now - now there's a chance none of us will make it out of this room. Not with John standing there with a taste for blood and violence. And even if we do make it out - here is a man who has now put himself in charge and, having had many a meeting with him, I'm not entirely sure his decisions will be what is the best for the group. "John - did you have anything to say to Dr. Platt?" Tina looked up at John. I didn't bother looking towards him. I could already tell he wanted to do to me what he'd already done to Darron. After all - I was part of the conversation last night so already the group doesn't trust me.

"Please stop this," Amy was crying but her words were ignored. Other members of the group were asking for the same but - again - their words fell upon deaf ears.

"John!" Tina's voice sounded alarmed. I looked at her and saw a look of panic in her face. I followed the gaze and couldn't help but scream when I saw what she was staring at. Others screamed too when they noticed Darron was up on his feet, standing behind John. His face was twisted and contorted in a way I'd never have thought possible. Blood tricking from his mouth still. Scissors poking out from his eyeball where they'd been left. A gargling noise from his throat. John jumped when he realised what everyone was looking at but it was wasted movement - he should have thrown himself across the desk and out of the way. Darron (is it still Darron) grabbed him with both hands and started to feverishly bite the other man's face. With each bite he tore another chunk of flesh off before helping himself to another. John was trying to push him away, whilst screaming, but made no progress.

I jumped to my feet and ran from the room. The others followed me although I hadn't instructed - nor wanted - them to do so. I ran down the dark corridor towards the fire escape and threw my body against the door. It didn't budge as I slammed into it. "What? No!" What was the point in a fire escape if the fucking thing was kept locked?

"What now?" a man called out from the back of the group. I didn't know 'what now'. This was the only way out of the building. The other route being blocked by Darron, I didn't fancy having to worm my way past him (or John for that matter).

"Up the stairs!" I pushed through the group and back down the corridor towards the spiral staircase. There was no way out that way. No access to the rooftop. Just a solitary room which was used for keeping older files. What it did have, though, was a window and - with any luck - that would be a way out for us. By the time we reached the stairs, John had stopped screaming. I feared the worst - Darron had killed him. But then I remembered the worst was still yet to come. If Darron had come back to life, what was to stop John from doing the same? At the top of the stairs I was the first into the small admin room. I waited by the door for the last person to enter before slamming it shut - but not before hearing the sound of groaning from downstairs. Not from one person but two. My heart skipped a beat as I realised what this meant.

"Now what?" Tina asked. I glared at her for the first time in my life. I confess to sometimes having 'out of place' thoughts about people but I always did it internally and was sure they'd never know what I was really thinking about them. But - this time - I couldn't hide my feelings. She had helped to get us into this position. More frustrating was the fact that Darron had informed us, before it kicked off, that it looked clear outside. Tina saw the look I gave her and backed away. For her sake, probably a wise move.

"There's no way out!" Amy helpfully pointed out, hyperventilating in the process.

"You need to control your breathing," I told her. My consultations with Amy had taught me she was prone to panic attacks periodically. Sometimes - from what she'd told me - they seemed to be for no reason at all. They'd just hit her out of the blue. If she were to have one now, at least there'd be a good reason.

A gush of cold wind blew into the room, sending a shiver down my spine in the process, as a man (whom I didn't know) opened the small window which overlooked the street. He stuck his head out and looked from side to side before pulling it back into the room.

"There's no way down!" he helpfully said.

Amy continued to hyperventilate as she clearly had the same thought that rushed through my own tired mind A single thought. We're all dead. A hand slammed against the door on which I leaned causing me to jump a foot in the air. A couple of the ladies, in the group, screamed out. We all knew what was on the other side of the door. I knew they'd come but - I have to be honest - I thought it would take them longer...A second hand banged on the door. The look on my face told everyone what I was thinking; I'm not sure how strong this door is. I'm not sure how many hits it will take before it finally gives way and they come crashing through. And when that happens - we're dead.

## Michael and Nicola

All things considered it wasn't a bad night. Certainly not as bad as I first feared it could have been. These things roaming the streets, I felt for sure there would be nowhere safe for us to seek shelter. As it turned out - we found brief sanctuary in an open garage not too soon after it had gotten dark. I had driven as far as I could before the roads became impassable; at least impassable with only the car's lights guiding us. As soon as I realised we couldn't get any further I knew it was time to take a break to rethink our plans. I back-tracked down the closest roads I could find until I found what I was looking for - an open (and practically empty) garage. Without hesitation I drove our car straight in. No sooner had the car stopped then I jumped out and slammed the garage door shut. A quick check of the door which linked to the actual house we'd found showed it to be locked which was the best possible scenario. We were trapped in our own little box and from what I had seen of these things - they weren't too good with doors. Nicola had asked what I was doing and I told her that we would be spending the night in the garage. She didn't seem to understand why we couldn't go into the house. I just told her it was safer where we were. Funny - all the things she'd seen during the day and she seemed more concerned about spiders than anything else we had witnessed. Of course I told her I'd keep her safe from the spiders. Besides which - the plan wasn't to sleep in the garage. Not literally. We were to remain in the car with the doors locked. That way, not only did those things have to get into the garage but they also had to get through the car doors too. It might not have been the most comfortable of nights but it was the safest I could make it - all things considered - and, to keep Nicola from being too scared, I kept the car's internal light on until she fell asleep. Sadly I couldn't fall asleep as easily as she seemed to. My brain overthinking things - worrying about every single detail of what I knew was coming my way the following morning (today).

The car was running low on fuel. We had enough for another fifty miles or so which would be fine under normal circumstances but given the amount of back-tracking we were doing I knew it wouldn't be enough. Not to get us all the way to the in-laws house. And then, of course, my mind was wondering what we were going to find when we got there. Would they be in? Would they be welcoming? Would it be as safe a haven as I had presumed? More importantly - if it wasn't to be the safe haven I believed - what would be the next move? Where else could we go?

Nicola stirred and slowly woke from her peaceful slumber. She was stretched out on the back seat of the car. I remember when she had first laid down, a feeling of jealousy that she was able to find some sort of comfort in here. I put the seat back, as far as I could without squashing her, but it still wasn't enough to give myself the necessary level of comfort I had wished for.

"Morning, sleepyhead!" I tried to keep things light and friendly. I tried to hide the fears I had swimming around the forefront of my mind. Not sure how well I did but at least I gave it a shot. She yawned and stretched. At least she had a good night. "You hungry?" I asked. She nodded. "I've got the best breakfast ever!" I leaned to the glove box and hit the release catch. The door dropped down, smacking me in the knees, revealing the sweets I had stashed a few days ago. I'd promised them to her yesterday, as a prize for getting to the car quietly, and clean forgotten. Just as well, though, for it meant we had a tasty breakfast. Tasty but not necessarily nutritious. I pulled the bag out and handed it over to Nicola who must have been thinking all of her Christmases had come at once. She snatched the bag and started scoffing them. I laughed. Should have taken a couple for myself though. "Ready to go and see Nanny and Granddad?" I asked. She nodded. All I had to do was open the garage door and we'd be on our way. I unlocked the car door and pushed it open. I told Nicola to, "Wait there."

I climbed from the car and stretched the aches from my joints; my back in particular. I'm too old to be trying to sleep in cars - at least my body feels as though that's what it is telling me. I approached the garage door and pulled the handle. I bent down and lifted the door up.

"Oh shit!"

Back in the car I heard Nicola panic as she saw what was waiting for us outside in the street. Dozens of infected - all of them seemingly lurching around with no clear sense of direction. One of them turned to us when Nicola screamed. And then - when one of them turned - more did too. By the time I got back to the driver's side of the car, and climbed in, they were already on the driveway in front of us. All of them looked hungry for us.

"Daddy, go!" Nicola cried out. I twisted the key in the ignition but nothing happened. What? No. Come on. I gave it another twist and still nothing. I thought back to the previous night and how long I must have left the interior light on for Nicola's peace of mind. Was that really enough to flatten the battery? One more go. Come on. Come on. I gave the key a twist. Still nothing. The engine was completely dead. "They're coming!" Nicola called out. I looked up. Shit. Shit. Shit. She was right. They were close. Need to shut the garage door - shut them out and us in.

"Wait here!" I called out to her as I climbed from the car - with much more haste this time. I charged across to the garage door and slammed it shut catching one of the infected's arms as he reached out for me. I took a few steps back with my eyes fixed on the garage door. The sound of the groaning from outside seeming to echo from where I was standing. Scratching noises as they fingered the cold metal door. A few more steps back but still I didn't look away. It's okay, though. Pretty sure they can't get in. Had they been able to, they would have already opened the door. I turned to my nervous daughter, "Get out of the car," I told her. She did as she was told and joined me where I was standing. "It's okay," I tried to reassure her, "it just means we stay here for a little longer..." I looked over to the door which lead through to the main house (most likely the kitchen). The only option I had was to go into the house. With any luck it would be empty (and secure). A place to leave Nicola for a while whilst I leave the house and try and find us another method of transport - or maybe a new battery? It's not an ideal plan but it's all I can think of. We need to get to the country for our best chance of survival. We need to get to the in-laws' house and - to do that - we need to get another car. I knew we should stick together but it's going to be dangerous out there. I can't risk taking Nicola with me. She'd be slower. More at risk. If this house is empty and secure well it would be best to leave her. Let her know that I'll be as quick as I can.

Ignoring the scratching on the garage door, I took Nicola by the hand and headed towards the internal door. Another try of the handle just to be sure it was locked proved that still to be the case. Here's hoping the door isn't as strong as it looks to be.

"Step back!" I told Nicola. She did as she was told and - no sooner had she done so - I started to kick the door as hard as I could. The noise my boot made against the wooden panel would surely attract more danger from outside but I didn't have a choice; not if we wanted to get in there.

"You're being noisy!" Nicola pointed out. Yes, I was. No choice. I kept kicking the door until - after what seemed an age - there was a cracking sound from near the handle. I felt a sense of relief. For a minute I had thought it wasn't going to budge. I gave it a few more kicks until I finally managed to splinter the area around the lock. A couple more kicks and the door slowly creaked open. I stopped - knackered - anxious about what would be standing there on the other side of the door. There was nothing. Just an empty kitchen. Another sense of relief washed over me but I knew it had the potential to be short-lived. Just because no one was standing there waiting didn't mean the house was empty or even secure. Hell, for all I knew the front door could have been left wide open and God knows how many of the infected could have wandered in. Don't think like that. Be optimistic. I nearly laughed out loud at the concept of optimism. That left yesterday morning when the shit first hit the fan. I turned to Nicola, "I need you to wait here, okay? I need to make sure the house is okay…" She nodded. I could tell she didn't want to stay there - alone - but I could also see she was apprehensive about following me in too. I gave her a kiss on the forehead and a little wink before I stepped into the kitchen via the broken door.

Part of me wanted to call out, to see if anyone was home, but I knew that the sound of my voice would only attract trouble if there was anything….else….home. Hell, for all I know, someone was waiting for me in one of the rooms with a gun, or something. Thank God this is England and not America. Less change of getting shot by some trigger happy home-owner worried that I'm trying to rob them. For a second my mind wandered as to whether this was happening in America too or whether it was just our country under attack from whatever this was. No time to think about that.

It's not important. Not yet. Doesn't help with my current predicament.

I made my way to the other side of the kitchen, towards the next door. I peered around the corner. Hallway was clear and the front door was shut. A good sign. Before proceeding I turned to the kitchen worktop and grabbed the biggest knife I could see. Some kind of carving knife. Good enough to do some damage. I caught sight of something glistening in the garden beyond the kitchen window. There was some kind of machete out there, sticking out of the mud next to some thick shrubbery. It was just a shame the garden was full of the infected - all meandering around. Thankfully, as of yet, none of them had spotted me. I turned back to Nicola. She was still in the garage, just beyond the doorway. I raised my finger to my lips - a signal for her to remain as quiet as she possibly could. She nodded.

With the knife held close to my body, I stepped into the hallway as quietly as I could. I listened closely to see if I could hear any panicked voices reacting to the sound of my dampened footsteps or the earlier kicking in of the door. Nothing. No voices and no groans. A good sign. I peeked into the first room I came to - nothing but a small toilet. I closed the door - so I definitely knew I had checked the room and proceeded, carefully, to the second room. The door was open so it wasn't hard to take a quick peek in; the living room. Again, thankfully empty. What I did notice, though, was that the room was in a state - as though someone had gone through it in a hurry, perhaps grabbing everything that had been important to them. The garage was open, as though it had been abandoned, so there was a good chance the owners had come home after the shit hit the fan and grabbed everything they could before hitting the road to try and find somewhere they believed to be a safer place to try and wait for help. The state of this place, it would make sense for that to be the case at least. Satisfied the room was empty, I closed the door as I stepped back into the hallway. No other rooms down here, just some stairs leading to the second floor of the house which I slowly started to make my way up - still with the knife held closely to my body although I was starting to relax a little.

At the top of the stairs I was faced with four rooms. The one closest to the top of the stairs was the bathroom and I could already see that it was empty. I closed the door on it and turned to the next room. Walking in I noticed it had been turned upside down just as the downstairs room had been. Another thought crossed my mind; it might not have been the owners who did this. Could have been people looting the house for any valuables. I dismissed the idea. No broken windows downstairs, no broken doors - other than the one I broke - and no other sign of forced entry. Just the owners leaving in a hurry with as many of their possessions they deemed necessary.

I wasn't paying much attention to the contents of the room but it was hard to miss the fact that it belonged to a young girl. A pink duvet was thrown over the bed, a couple of dolls were left lying on the floor - clearly not important enough to be saved. Some clothes left hanging in an open cupboard with others on the floor next to it where they must have fallen or been thrown. I stepped from the room and closed the door. Two down, two to go...I headed for the next room; another bedroom of similar size to the last. No doubt, going from some of the clothes on the floor and ornaments dotted around the room, the parents' room. Same story here as with the other rooms - emptied in a hurry, more importantly - empty of people, both living or dead. One room to go. I stepped out and closed the door behind me before turning to the last room. This is it then.

I made my way to the end of the hallway and carefully peered into the room. Just because it is the last room to check - doesn't mean I can get complacent about what may or may not be in there. A study. A computer monitor on a table and an overturned chair. The actual computer unit was missing. Only cables remained suggesting it was even there to begin with. I guess the owner couldn't afford to be without some of the information stored on the hard-drive. Funny the things people consider important during moments of crisis. Personally I'd have left it. Jesus - what am I talking about - I left without taking anything other than my daughter. Everything else was fine to abandon.

Satisfied the house was clear I checked out of the window into the street beyond. The road seems to have a large amount of infected out there. A lot of them still swarming towards our garage door by the looks of things. Thankfully they don't seem to be making any progress towards breaching it but it's hard to tell from this angle. We can't stay here for long. I stepped back from the window so as to remain unseen by any of them. Last thing I need is for them to be banging on the front door when - sooner or later - I'm going to have to dart out of it as I go in search of transportation.

I tucked the knife between my belt and jeans and headed down the stairs, back towards the garage where my daughter is hiding.

"It's okay to come in," I said as I walked through the kitchen. She had her back to me and the sound of my voice made her jump. She turned to me and ran in through the broken doorway.

"They're still trying to get in," she said, referring to the creatures outside. She ran into my arms and I couldn't help but to give her a tight hug. I just wish I could take the two of us away from all of this in the blink of an eye. Surely as a family we'd been through enough without the need for this too?

"They can't get in. It's okay. We're safe." Technically not a lie. Although we're not out of the woods yet we are, for all intents and purposes, safe. "Look, there are people outside…"

"Dead people?" she asked.

I was kind of hoping she didn't know that's what they were but figured - as she asked - there was no point in lying to her. With what was happening out there, she needed to be prepared for what we were likely to run into. Lying to her now would just make it worse in the long-run. "Yes," I told her. "Listen, we need to go upstairs and keep away from the windows, okay? You think you can do that?" She nodded. "We don't want them knowing we're in here."

"What about the ones at the garage door?" she asked.

"They'll get bored and go. But we don't want any more showing up do we?" She shook her head. "Good. Well, okay, this way then...I think you'll like one of the rooms up there," I told her. I gave her a little smile and lead the way up the stairs with her following closely behind.

<u>Ted</u>

Harold slammed the door shut behind me. I couldn't help but
feel he did it harder than strictly necessary in order to try and
attract trouble for me. Had the shoe been on the other foot, I
guess I would have done the same just to fuck him over. I
was glad I didn't give him the option of coming with me as I
headed down the empty alleyway. Oh ye of little faith. I knew
the alleyway would be clear. Well, okay, I didn't but - fuck it -
nothing to lose. I got to the end of it within seconds and -
before I knew it - I was standing on the edge of the high
street. In front of me - just a few yards or so - the R.D.Fs
were still trying to get into the front of the store by banging
and clawing on the window. I figured as Harold tried to 'help'
me out, it was only fair that I extended him the same level of
courtesy and I knew just the thing to do it with.

I stepped back into the alleyway - out of sight - and picked up
a brick from a small amount of rubble which had been
hidden there by someone too lazy to dispose of it properly.
Normally people like that piss me off. You know, like it's that
hard to bin something. But not today. Today I was grateful
there was a lazy fuck nearby. With brick in hand, I dashed
back into the street and - without really thinking about it -
charged towards the backs of the R.D.Fs. When I felt I was
close enough I aimed towards the store's window and

launched the brick. It flew through the air - almost in slow-motion it felt - and hit the pane of glass. Immediately the glass shattered as the brick crashed through into the racking. Just as planned, the brick was first through the window followed by the first of the Rotten Dead Fucks. The store's alarm rang through the streets and - by the time I turned around - I saw more of the R.D.Fs on the horizon, all stumbling their way towards the sound. I laughed as I cast a quick look up to the flat window - above the store - and saw Harold standing there with a panic-stricken look on his face. I flipped him the bird and took a bow. Fuck you, Harold. Fuck you very much!

I turned and quickly ran in the direction which seemed to be the clearest of danger, laughing as I did. With what just happened - I can't help but feel this situation we find ourselves in...This situation is good for people like me and, not only that, I think I'm going to enjoy it! There are no rules. There is no right and wrong. There is only survival of the fittest and I believe, in times like these, the 'fittest' tend to be the people such as myself; the ones with nothing to lose and everything to gain. The ones with a screw or two loose. If anything, knowing the world had gone fuck up, I actually felt freer than I had done so before. The thoughts I had - the troubling ones about what I wanted to do to people - they no longer seemed to bother me and as I continued to run towards a housing estate it made me realise that it was never the act of my fantasies which troubled me but rather it was the potential for getting caught and ending up in the shit.

As I weaved my way effortlessly through another small cluster of R.D.Fs I couldn't help but think - I welcome this new world with both arms outstretched. I embrace it. I could be a fucking King. People like me - the people labelled as damaged, dangerous, demented and sick - we're the ones who will survive. We're the ones who will go all the way. We're the ones who will be your leaders. You may as well prepare yourself to already bow down to me. Hail to the king.

## Dr. Platts

I pushed my way through the nervous group and reached the window. I knew this was the only way out of the room - if the door wasn't usable which, going by the relentless banging, it isn't - but I didn't ever recall it being so small. Certainly not a standard sized window. Maybe big enough for Amy, the smallest of the group, to fit through but the rest of us would struggle. And then, of course, there are a couple of us who simply would not even begin to fit through. With my head through the window I knew I could squeeze myself out but - looking around - there was nothing but a straight drop to the concrete below. There were no nearby ledges to get a hold of, there was nothing. I muttered a swear word under my breath. Even if the drop didn't kill us - and there was a good chance it wouldn't - there was no way we would get away without breaking at least one bone (most likely an ankle) and given what's happening out there - that would surely end up leading to our deaths anyway when we find ourselves unable to get away from oncoming danger. I muttered another swear word.

Tina had pushed her way through to me and was screaming in my ear for what we were to do next. "Well now what? You lead us up here," she said, "so what's the plan? Or did you just lead us to a room with no way out?"

I turned back to the room. Two of the male members of the group had their hands pressed against the door in an effort to stop the force being applied to the other side breaking it down. Other members of the group had gathered, facing the door, in the further possible corner of the room and Amy and Tina were staring at me - wide-eyed and desperate for some kind of answer from me. I didn't have one though. I had nothing for them. Tina sensed my lack of answers being a sign that I didn't have any to give.

"You've killed us," she hissed. Her voice full of the venom that I'd previously heard in the waiting area of the building - when she was egging John on with each punch he put upon Darron. "She's killed us!" she alerted the group, "There is no way out of here. We're all as good as dead." I felt the eyes of the group rest upon me. No. This wasn't my fault. If people had listened to me we'd all still be downstairs. We'd be preparing to make our run to wherever we were going to end up going for. We'd all be safe and - more to the point - we'd all be alive. None of us would have witnessed the vicious attack. None of us would have blood on our hands. Tina made a sudden lunge towards me but I successfully managed to move out of the way. Purely on reaction I hit her, open-palmed, across the face. If she wanted confrontation, knowing what was waiting for us on the other side of the door growing more and more impatient, I'd gladly oblige her. She regained her composure and turned back to me with a look of shock upon her face, along with a red mark from the slap. Hardly surprising considering my hand is stinging painfully.

"You did this, you crazy bitch! If you hadn't gone to the group and run your mouth off about stuff which was, quite frankly, none of your business and certainly not decided upon then Darron and John would both still be alive. We all stood there and watched what John did without doing anything to stop him so, in a way, we all have blood on our hands but you - you have the most. You caused the argument and you nodded to John to do what he did. You did. Not us. So if you want to stand here and play the blame game, I suggest you reassess who you try and pin the blame on. And so what if Darron, and I for that matter, had decided to go it alone. We don't owe you anything. We don't owe any of you anything…" I stopped. The room was looking at me. I didn't dare look around at people. I didn't dare see their reaction to my outburst. I concentrated my glare upon Tina whose eyes were filling with tears - wondering where she'd take the outburst.

"You couldn't just leave us!" she blurted out. "What were we going to do? Where were we going to go?" All of this happened because she was scared of being left alone? Really? All of this happened because her worried mind had already taken the conversation she had heard as truth. Jesus H. Christ. The stupid little woman. "I have to get back to my dad!" she said. She started to cry. I didn't care though. I didn't feel sympathy for her. Maybe I'd spent too long listening to various sob stories? Maybe I had only just given up caring. I'm not sure. "He'll be scared."

"Do you really think," I put the boot in, "that if your father is still alive…Do you really think any of the rest of us would want to swing by your house to go and fetch him?" I shook my head. "We wouldn't. We'd want to go to the safest place we could think of and we'd want to do so without extra baggage." I knew my words were harsh but I wasn't about to apologise. She'd annoyed me more than anyone else I'd ever met. Dear Tina, the meek little woman. "Now if you do not have anything sensible to suggest to the group, anything which may help us out of this situation, I'd kindly ask you to get off my back and shut the fuck up." I turned away from her and looked at the rest of the group. They all looked scared. I can't blame them. It hadn't been more than two days and already people were turning on each other and that was before we faced the rest of the world. Hardly the best of starts.

"We could throw the boxes out of the window," Amy suggested. I turned to her to hear her out but - I have to admit - I was already at a loss as to where she was going with this. "If we just drop them," she continued, "they'd gradually build up..." my mind caught up with where she was headed, "...and - if we jump - it would offer some support. Something a little softer to land on."

The room was filled with years and years worth of filing - all stashed in cardboard boxes designed for such a purpose. Each one with the date and year scrawled across it in thick black marker. Government regulations insisted they were kept on premises for x amount of years before being securely disposed of. Whilst Amy's suggestion certainly wasn't foolproof or even as safe as I'd have liked it to be - it was the best option we currently had. Other than opening the door and wandering into the path of the two things trying to come through the other side - it was the only option.

"It might work," a man piped up. I looked across to where the voice came from and my heart sank. Her plan might work for some of us but not everyone. Some would have to stay behind. This man was one of them. His facial expression clearly suggested he knew he'd be left behind but he still made his way over to the closest of the boxes. With some effort he picked it up and dropped it through the window. As the box fell to the floor the lid flew off and confidential notes, and other paperwork, flew through the air. So much for doctor / patient confidentiality. "And you can come back, with help, for those who can't fit through the window," he said. A hint of 'hope' in his tone.

"Of course." I made no promises. We both knew - whoever made it through the window and down onto the floor safely - no one would be going back for anyone. It was very much a dog eat dog world out there now.

One by one a chain started to form between the people who weren't tied up propping the door up. Each member passing the boxes from person to person until it reached the man who was dropping them from the window to the floor below.

"How many should we do?" Amy asked.

"All of them," I suggested. For our best chance of making this work, we needed the maximum amount of cushioning below us and I was well aware that the more people dropped down to them - the more they'd start to flatten.

"You guys need to go faster," one of the door props called over, "it's starting to splinter over here!"

## Michael and Nicola

Nicola was on the bed - with its pink duvet set - toying with one of the abandoned dolls. She wasn't really playing with it as such, just fiddling with it as there was little else to do. I'd gone through the upstairs of the house, closing the curtains, and I'd snuck back into the kitchen to raid the near-empty shelves for whatever food was left behind; not that the previous occupants had left much for us. At least - not much food that didn't require any form of cooking.

"What's that you've found there?" I asked from the doorway where I was watching Nicola. I only asked because I was trying to act normal. I think Nicola knew that too but she played along.

"Just a doll. I found it on the floor."

"Does the doll have a name?"

"Victoria."

Named after her mother. I couldn't help but wonder whether she was still thinking about seeing her mum out there in the garden. It was hard to say goodbye the first time, I can't imagine what must have gone through her mind when she saw her out there on the middle of the lawn.

"Nice name," I said, skirting around the fact it was her mother's name. I wasn't ready for any possible conversations about why her mum - my wife - had come back and, more to the point, why we had just left her there. There was a good chance Nicola knew the reasons, she wasn't stupid after all, but I still didn't want to open the floor up to discussion. Not yet. Everything is too raw.

"Listen you know we can't stay here, don't you?" I tentatively approached the subject I was dreading discussing (for more than one reason). "We need to get to Nanny and Granddad's house."

"I know."

"And to do that we need a new car." I sat down on the edge of the bed. I didn't want to leave her alone but I didn't have a choice. If I go out there alone, I have more chance to get what I need. I can't watch my daughter, my own surroundings and keep an eye out for a possible vehicle too. I knew there weren't masses of the infected out there but there was enough to run into trouble if I made a wrong turn or put myself in a corner. I needed to be alert and concentrate on what I was doing. "I'm going to need you to be brave," I continued, "and stay here whilst I pop out and get us a new car."

Nicola immediately looked up, panic on her face, "I don't want to stay here by myself."

"You have to. I can't take you with me, it's dangerous out there. You'll be safer here," my mind started playing the bastard game of 'what if'. What if I ran into trouble? What if I got bitten? What if I couldn't make it back for whatever reason? She'd be alone, trapped. I tried to shake the poisoned thoughts from my mind. I didn't need those things floating around in there. Not now. I can't afford to be distracted. And I can't afford to make the decision to take her with me. "And I won't be long," I told her. A silly thing to say. It was impossible to say how long it would take. It was even impossible to say whether I'd find what I was looking for - what I desperately needed to get my daughter to the safety she deserved. "You just need to hang tight here. Just stay in this room," I told her. "You have food, you have some toys you can play with and - before you know it - I'll be back to get you."

"You will come back?"

"Oh my darling, of course. Just let them try and stop me." I smiled at her. She smiled back but I could see she was nervous about the situation.

"Well when do you have to leave?" she asked.

"The sooner I go, the sooner I am back."

"And then we'll go to Nanny's?" she asked. I smiled at her. She has such an innocence about her and it breaks my heart to know that - minute by minute - this situation is robbing her of it. I couldn't help but wonder if I'd ever manage to get it back to her. I leaned down to where she was sitting and kissed the top of her head.

"Can daddy have a hug before he goes?" I asked. She didn't need asking twice. She jumped up and threw her arms around me as though scared it would be the last time she ever saw me. I held her tight. Didn't want to let her go. Didn't want to leave her. I felt myself well up. Need to hold it together. Need to be strong for the both of us. I heard that she wasn't doing so well at keeping calm. She quietly wept as I held her. I don't need to leave right this minute. A couple more minutes won't hurt. A couple more minutes to just enjoy the peace and love between us. "Love you," I reminded her. She whispered back to me that she loved me too. I gave her another tight squeeze before I released her. "Okay, remember what I said, stay upstairs and away from the window and I'll be back as quickly as I can. Okay?" she nodded. I thought for a moment and then tried to hand her the knife I'd earlier taken from the kitchen when I was first looking around the house. "And if anyone comes in - any of those people out there - I want you to run as fast as you can. But if you're stuck in here - stick this in them." She looked at me with a confused expression and I couldn't say I blamed her. It's not the usual thing a father tells his daughter to do. She didn't take the knife so I put it on the bed. She knew it was there and - hopefully - she wouldn't need it anyway. I gave her another kiss on the cheek before I stood up. It's now or never.

I looked out of the bedroom window, peering from behind the curtain, down into the garden below. The machete is still staring at me, beckoning me to go and get it but there are too many of the infected down there to make it a wise move.

One trip and I'd be brown bread. I left the room, giving
Nicola a little wave as I did so, before heading through to the
front bedroom. Same thing - a quick look out of the window
from behind the curtains. The garage seems to be holding
the attention of most of the infected, down there, but I know
it won't be the same story if one of them catches sight of me
leaving the house. When one sees something, it's as though
they all see it. Before you know it - you have a dozen, or so,
on your back. I'm just thankful they're not fast.

I noticed a car parked in the drive of the house opposite me.
No guarantees there are any keys in the house but I'm
guessing it's a good place to start. I noticed the front door
was wide open. That wasn't a good sign as it increased the
chances of some of those things being in there - whether
they be the owner of the house or they just meandered in
from the street. Well, no choice, really. I'm fully aware of the
fact I'm going to have to get my hands dirty at some point.

There were a couple of infected lurching on the street
between the two houses and one in the drive of the opposite
house. Apart from that, from what I could see at this angle, it
looked relatively clear. I closed my eyes. Thoughts of my
daughter flashed through my mind. Her pretty smile.
Watching her playing in the garden last summer happily
singing to herself as I prepared a barbecue for the family. I'm
doing this for her. I'm doing this for her. I released the corner
of the curtain and let it flap back before leaving the room. I
hurried down the stairs and through to the kitchen. A quick
search of the sides and I grabbed another knife to replace
the one I'd left Nicola. Funny - I rarely let her use the scissors

when she was doing her arts and crafts and there I am leaving her with a sodding great knife. Desperate times. Another knife in hand, I turned from the room and headed towards the front door. A similar set up to the one I had left behind, in my own home, in that it had narrow windows either side of the door so I could see out. The coast was clear. Okay. No messing around. I just need to open the door and run as fast as I can. Get to the other side of the road and into the house. Shut the door as quickly (and quietly) as possible and then go from room to room cleaning the place out. Then - and only then - can I set about finding any possible keys for the car. Well - on the plus side - it sounds as though it's simple enough. I took a few deep breaths and grabbed a hold of the Yale door lock. This is it.

I knew she couldn't hear me, from where she was hiding, but I said it anyway, "I love you, Nic..."

I flipped the lock and quietly opened the door to the harsh world beyond.

## Dr. Platts

Most of the boxes were on the hard floor outside of the building now. Some had retained their contents and others had spilled them across the road where the wind had helped to carry them further. Amy was the obvious choice to send through the window first; she was the lightest after all. If she didn't make it down safely then none of us would (not that I told her that). I grabbed her by the shoulders and made sure she looked me in the eyes, "You need to run as soon as you land."

Amy looked towards the window, "What if I break something in the fall?"

I pulled her back to me, "You won't."

"You're sure?" Of course I wasn't sure but she didn't need to know that. She just needed to get down there and run in whatever direction she fancied. "What do I do when I am down?" she asked.

"You just run."

"I'll wait for you?" she asked. "I'll wait for all of you," she looked around the group. All of them were looking as concerned as I felt. I waited for her to look back to me again. "I'll wait," she repeated.

124

"No. No, you won't. You wait for nothing. As soon as you can, you start running - do you hear me?" The noise of the boxes being flung from the window had already alerted some of the infected to the fact we were in the building and we could see them making their way up the street - from wherever they came from - towards where we were hiding. We needed to hit the floor running.

"Where do I go?" I could see the panic in Amy's face at the prospect of being alone but if she waited down there, for the rest of us to join her, she'd be swarmed by the infected. Chances are she'd even be one of them by the time the rest of us made it down. With regards to her question though, I'd already thought of an answer. It just came to me, out of the blue, whilst we were lining the streets with confidential reports and broken boxes. We needed to make our way to the supermarket. It didn't matter which one. But we could make it secure and we could live there for as long as it took the promised help to find us. "Where do I go?" she asked again.

"The supermarket." I turned to address the whole room. The ones, at least, who would be able to get out of the window. "We need to go to the supermarket. Once there we can make the building secure. We'll have safety. We'll have food. It's our best shot." No one argued with me. Most weren't even looking at me; the group was divided - some worried about the door holding out and some concerned about dropping from the second story of the building onto a pile of boxes as though they were meant to be pillows. I turned to

Amy, aware that the door wasn't going to hold the infected out forever, "You need to go."

Two of the men helped Amy out of the window. They took an arm each and held her as she backed out. The plan was simple; they'd lower her as much as they could and then - with a head's up - they'd drop her the remaining distance. The size of the window didn't allow them to lean out of the window together - not completely - but it was better than nothing.

"Please don't drop me!" Amy was whimpering as they lowered her from the window. I couldn't watch. I turned back to the door as it continued to buckle and strain from the force exerted on the other side. I heard Amy suddenly scream and span back around to the window. The two men came back in - empty handed. I dashed across to the window and leaned out. Amy was on the floor. Boxes were crumpled around her but - other than that - she was safe and sound. She clambered to her feet and stumbled down the remaining boxes. "I'm okay," she shouted. I grimaced as soon as the first words escaped her mouth. It was bad enough that she'd screamed on the way down but - to shout again - it did nothing but attract more attention.

"Run!" I whispered down to her. "Meet at the supermarket!" She nodded and started off in the direction of the supermarket. It was a fair trek away, especially on foot, but if we were careful we'd all make it there. I looked around the street and noticed a lot of the infected had turned their attention to following Amy. She had a good head start so -

chances are - she'd be fine as long as she was careful. It was funny but, for the first time ever, I actually felt as though I'd properly helped someone.

A scream from behind made me spin on the spot. The door had fractured and both Darron and John had spilled into the room. They'd fallen on top of the two men who'd been propping the door up and were already biting and scratching at them. The man under John screamed out loud as John's hands disappeared into the man's stomach. By the time they came back from within the gut, they had handfuls and handfuls of intestine. Tina made a dash for the window.

"Let me out!" she screamed. Without waiting for any help, or support, she clambered through the narrow gap and disappeared with a shriek. Unlike when Amy went through the window - TIna's screaming continued long after she should have hit the cardboard boxes. I didn't need to look. I already knew what it'd meant. Something had broken. The group backed up to the window. By now I was the closest so I wasted no time in scrambling through it myself. I looked down - a long way up - and saw Tina on the floor below. Her leg had twisted in the complete wrong direction. From this stance, I could see a bone fragment poking through her broken skin. Please God let me land safely. I closed my eyes and let go of the window ledge, plummeting to the floor below; the cardboard boxes in particular. The landing was painful but certainly not as painful as it could have been. I clawed my way out of the middle of the pile and landed next to where Tina was still screaming for someone to help her. I looked up, adrenaline surging through my veins, and immediately noticed the unwanted attention her cries for help had received. "Please!" she screamed at me, "Please help me!" I looked at her at disbelief. This woman - the one who set these events in motion - begging me for help as though she really believed I was going to risk my life to save her own miserable existence. Someone screamed from the window ledge. I looked up in time to see another of the smaller girls poking from out of the window. A pair of hands were wrapped around her face. Even from down here I heard the snap of her neck as the hands twisted her head the opposite way around. I closed my eyes at the repulsive sight. By the time I opened them - the woman was no longer in the window. I pulled myself up to my feet and went to make a run for the supermarket as agreed. Tina reached up and grabbed a hold of the trouser leg of my suit. "Please don't leave me here!" More screams from beyond the window. No others will be following me out. At least - not alive.

"Get off me!" I kicked her off with the heel of my shoe and made off in the same direction Amy had run. I surprised myself when I didn't look back. Not even when her screaming went up a notch as - I presume - the infected reached where she was crippled. I know I'm supposed to help people in my profession but - as of right now - I've quit. Especially if they're quick to stab me in the back.

## Amy

Amy didn't stop running despite every joint screaming for her to do so. Every time she looked behind her she was sure she could see more of the infected. They weren't close enough to cause her any trouble but she knew - she knew - if she stopped for a moment, to catch her breath, they'd be on top of her ripping into her flesh with both teeth and nail.

She turned a corner and felt her heart sink when she noticed the surging horde of infected pacing the roads before her. With still so far to go - to get to the supermarket - she couldn't help but panic. What if she didn't make it there? Or what if she did make it there but she was too late, despite the head-start? She'd get there only to find the place barricaded shut, with no way in, and still with the horde right on her tail.

"Please, God, give me a break!" she whined despite knowing, God wasn't listening anymore, if He ever had been paying attention in the first place. Just as she was mentally mapping out her route, the sound of a car horn alerted her. It came from behind her, from the hordes she was running from. She span around and felt a wave of relief rush through her at the sight of a large 4x4 speeding towards her - swerving erratically from side to side, hitting as many of the infected as humanly possible. The car horn sounded again as the car drove over the skull of a downed undead - spreading blackened brain over the tread of the tyre and grit of the concrete. Amy waved towards the car in an effort to flag it down. "Please! Over here!" she shouted. She didn't care that her screams would attract any of the horde. She didn't have to care - not with help speeding towards her. Speeding. Swerving. Amy's eyes went wide when it dawned on her - the 4x4 wasn't here to help her. It wasn't there to help anyone. The driver merely out on a jolly jaunt to see how much trouble he could cause - how many infected he could kill. Before she could react - the front of the vehicle slammed into her. She managed to stay there for a moment, wide-eyed panic in her eyes and blood pouring from her mouth from damage sustained, but it wasn't long before she slipped from the driver's view. The 4x4's suspension stopped the driver from feeling any hint of discomfort as it bounced over her body.

As the vehicle pummelled into the next cluster of the infected, Amy opened her now-cloudy eyes. She didn't get up. Her body was too broken. Instead she started clawing her way aimlessly across the road, groaning as she did, dragging her mangled legs behind her.

## Ted

Absolutely-fucking-brilliant! I couldn't help but laugh as I
watched the truck mow the girl down. I mean - brilliant but
also a damned shame because she was a tasty piece of gash
right there. And to think here I was wondering whether I was
alone in this shit-hole town and then - boom - two survivors
within a couple of seconds of each other. One survivor now.
Glad I hadn't tried to wave them down, try and make friends
with them just as I'd made friends with Harold. I stepped out
from the shadows where I'd been watching the drama
unfold, wondering how to get past the rotting dead fucks,
and ran in the direction of the cul-de-sac just off the main
road. Not so many R.D.Fs to worry about now, thanks to my
friend in the truck. As I entered the cul-de-sac I couldn't help
but feel my spirits rise further. Some nice looking houses
down this road which - I'm sure - will be filled with rich
pickings. To think, I've lived in this area most of my life and
yet I don't think I've ever been down this road before. Funny
how things turn out.

## Nicola

Nicola was sitting on the floor, next to the bed, huddled into
a little ball. The knife was where her father had left it, on the
side of the bed. The doll was where she'd dropped it when

she went to give him a hug goodbye. She was still whimpering - not because she was scared of what was outside, that went without saying, but more so because she was worried about her dad. She got up and cautiously left the bedroom. She hesitated there, in the doorway, before she nervously made her way down the landing and towards the bedroom which overlooked the main room. The curtains were still shut (just as her father had left them). She hurried across the room and stopped by the curtain where she froze, her head tilted to the side from where she was straining to hear something (anything).

Groans and gargled noises from, she guessed, down by the garage. Some kind of alarm was sounding off in the distance but she wasn't able to say whether it was a car or house alarm. Maybe even a shop alarm. Something thudded from somewhere downstairs and she jumped. She twisted herself towards the door - nervous that someone was about to burst in. No one came. She paused. No further thuds or bangs. No one there. No one coming. She breathed a sigh of relief and turned back to the curtain. She desperately wanted to see if she could see her dad out there. If only a glimpse of him. Something just to let her know that he was out there and - more to the point - that he was okay. Nervously she reached out with her hand and pulled back the curtain. Not a lot - just enough to see out of.

She peeped out. Across the road, at the house opposite, she noticed a large swarm of the undead crowding around the front door. There was a car, on the driveway of the same house, with the alarm ringing out as though it had been disturbed. Headlights flashing to warn people someone had been interfering with it - on the off-chance on one heard the alarm. Despite the number of undead clawing at the (closed) front door the house - Nicola felt a wave of relief. She knew there was a good chance the noise, and general disturbance, was down to her father.

## Michael

I fell back against the wall once the security chain was fastened on the front door. Out of breath. I couldn't help but thank God for ensuring the door had been open. Had it not been I would have been dead. I can't believe how quickly I was surrounded out there. One minute everything had been relatively clear - I had tried the car door setting the alarm went off - and next thing they were all on top of me. I only hope the keys are in here somewhere. I heard the infected scrambling at the front door. I also hoped there was a back door out of here and that it is clear from any of the undead. Jesus. I can't believe how quickly those things were there. Watching them, from a distance, and they're deceptively slow but - yeah - I won't be under estimating...I froze as something smashed in the next room down the hallway. Oh shit.

## Nicola

Nicola couldn't take her eyes away from the front door across the road. Her heart was in the back of her throat as she desperately waited to see some sign of her dad there. Quickly she cast her eyes from window to window of the property in the hope of seeing him standing there - perhaps looking to see if he could spot a way out and back to the car. She knew there was no way he'd get to the car. Not with all of them crowding the front of the house. No clear path. It was too dangerous. She paused a moment, her young mind frantically trying to think of a way to help her father. And then it struck her. She needed to create a diversion - something to turn their attention away from where he was hiding, something to give him the necessary space to get to the car before coming back to get her.

Ted

I landed hard on my arse as the fence gave way under my weight. How embarrassing. Thankfully there didn't seem to be anyone around to spot my little accident. Fucking gate was locked so it wasn't as though I had had much of a choice. I wasn't doing it to appear macho or try and be the Action Man. I was climbing the fence as I figured it would be easier to go from garden to garden as opposed to running down the street - out in the open. I sat up and realised I wasn't alone. A garden full of rotting dead fucks. Brilliant. Perhaps the road would have been a fuck sight easier. I quickly scrambled to my feet and scanned the area to try and determine the best direction to make a run for it. Don't really want to go back. Back is never good. Always need to push forward. That's my motto in life. Don't look back. Just move forward. Make a decision and stick with it. Too many fuckers out there pick and choose what they want only to change their...Oh hello. In scanning the immediate area I noticed a nice looking machete sticking out of ground. I couldn't help but smile. Bad-ass.

Without hesitation I scrambled towards it (more or less on all fours) and pulled it from the damp mud. In the nick of time too as one of the rotting dead fucks dared to make a move for me with a sudden lunge. With perfect precision I made sure it would never lunge again as the tip of the machete blade went through its mushy skull. One final groan from it. Fucking sweet. I should have found me one of these ages ago. I ripped the blade from the fucker's head and it dropped to the floor completely lifeless - and still which was a bonus. No need to run with this little weapon. At least not when there's not too many of the R.D.Fs to contend with. Might as well get some practice in for when the going gets really tough.

I couldn't help but laugh as I squared up to the next rotting fuck who dared approach me. Bring it, bitch. Feeling a little more confident I span on the spot with my arm outstretched. The blade of the machete a mere extension of my hand. With a perfect aim the sharp blade connected with the head of the R.D.F and sliced through it as though it were hot knife through butter. The head flew from the shoulders, spinning through the air and spraying blood all over the show. It landed on the floor. Rude not to go for the touchdown. I charged the still chomping head and gave it the mightiest toe punt I could muster. Hurt my toe in the process but totally worth it as the fucking thing easily cleared the fence. I heard it land with a thud as I turned my attention to the next target. I couldn't help but think back to the news reports - not one of them mentioned the perks of having a machete.

Had they done so, perhaps there'd be more people fighting alongside me? I swung the blade at the next reachable neck.

## Michael

I slowly walked down the hallway. I held the knife close to my side, ready to lunge at whatever was in the other room. I hoped it was the sound of a person hiding from me. Maybe even a cat knocking something down? Whatever it was - I just preyed it wasn't one of the infected. At the doorway now and I slowly peered around the corner, into the room. My heart skipped a beat when I saw one of the infected standing there, in the opposite corner of the room, with its back to me. It hadn't heard me - thank God. It was just standing there, the occasional gargled noise gasping from its mouth. The stench in the room nearly made me gag but I managed to hold it together. Can't go making a sound. Not when it is so close and I'm limited with places I can run to. I need to catch it by surprise to take it down. One of them, by themselves, probably wouldn't cause me too many problems if it did suddenly turn but it wasn't something I wanted to risk - not with my daughter across the road waiting for me to take her to safety. Slowly I made my way across the room towards where it was standing. I raised the tip of the knife towards the back of its head. Need to thrust forward hard and fast - enough pressure to get through the skull and into the brain. I was within an arm's length now. That stench - something I'd never be able to forget no matter how much I wanted to. I wanted to close my eyes for what I was to do but I couldn't. I needed to be sure I hit the right spot. I needed to be sure I was going to kill it.

"God forgive me," I muttered. The sound of my voice alerted the infected to my presence but it didn't matter now. It was too late. I thrust forward before it had even half turned to face me and grimaced as the knife went through the skull. The tip poked out of the other side. The infected, a woman, gave a final snarl before she fell silent. Definitely dead. I pulled the knife back and the body slumped to its knees before falling forward - face first through a glass coffee table. With the danger out of the way, the smell hit me hard and I gagged. A second later and I threw up onto the floor, next to the dead body. Stop it. Get a grip. I wiped the puke from the sides of my mouth and spat the remnants onto the floor. Need to get up. Need to be sure there aren't any more of them in the house and then I need to find the keys. Please God let them be in here somewhere. And if you're really listening - please let them be in an obvious place.

Nicola

Nicola opened the curtain letting the daylight spill into the room in the process. She squinted from the sudden brightness but soon shook it off. The view outside, in the main road, terrified her but she knew she couldn't ignore it. She needed to get the attention away from where her father was holed-up. The sooner she made it clear for him, the sooner he'd be able to come and collect her. Where other children her age may have hesitated to do anything, Nicola showed no such hesitation as she opened the window. Her plan as simple as it could have been; make enough noise to ensure the infected heard her. She leaned out of the window and hoped that her dad was ready to come home.

## Ted

I was covered head to foot in blood by the time I had worked my way through the garden. I peeked over the next fence when I realised I could hear the sound of groans coming from beyond. Shit loads of RDFs. What is it with these fucks and their garden parties? Might actually be easier going down the front way so I made my way round to the front of the house via a narrow side alley. I didn't charge out into the open. Not that fucking stupid despite what people have told me before. Wonder where they are now. Probably dead. Hopefully dead. Cunts. Immediately to my right I noticed a fuck load of Rotting Dead Fucks banging and scrabbling to get into a garage. Wonder what's got their attention? The sound of a girl screaming made me jump (and the RDFs stop what they were doing). I looked up and saw a young girl leaning from the upstairs window of the house. The RDFs noticed her too and staggered their way to the front door. Worse than that - for the girl - I noticed another group of RDFs across the road turn around to see what the commotion was. Time for Ted to play the Samaritan...

## Michael

Upstairs in the seemingly empty house, I recognised the scream immediately - even with the sound of the car alarm still sounding off. I dashed towards a window in the front of the property - didn't even check my surroundings before bursting into the room. Luckily it was empty. Looking out of the window, my heart stopped as I felt my world come crashing down around me. Nicola was leaning from the window in the house I'd left her in. She screamed again. What? Why? Had something got into the house with her? Was she in danger? I banged on the window. She saw me - not sure if that was because of the banging or because she was keeping an eye out - and waved. She's waving? Can't be in danger then. Not imminent danger anyway. I reached for the window latch and lifted it. A quick shove and the window swung open.

I called out, "What's wrong?" Not sure if she could hear me. I couldn't hear her clearly enough because of the fucking car alarm but she was shouting something back to me. She beckoned me back towards her and pointed down to the front of the house I was in. I looked down and realised what she was doing. A distraction. The infected which had been trying to get in through the front were headed for the other house. Her house. Shit. What have you done? I looked back up to my daughter and called out again, "Close the window and hide!" I shouted. The car alarm was drowning my voice out so I called again, "CLOSE THE WINDOW AND HIDE!" Some of the infected heard me and turned back but the others continued forward. Shit. Shit. Shit. I needed to hurry and find the keys. If the infected got in here - I'd be able to fight them off or, at the very least, find another way out. If they get in there...Doesn't bear thinking about. I went to call out again, another last ditch attempt to tell her to hide, but the words didn't come out. Blind panic set in as I realised she wasn't alone in the room. Someone was standing behind her.

I screamed for her to turn around; a scream loud enough for her to hear me. I saw her turn around as the shadow approached her.

Nicola

"You need to stop all the noise," Ted said. He was standing in the doorway, blocking Nicola's way out of the bedroom. The machete was still in his hand, dripping black blood onto the cream carpet. "You're attracting all sorts of trouble," he continued. "Now the bad news is we can't leave via the front door but the good news is - I've made the back way, the way I came in, pretty much clear of any trouble." Nicola saw the machete in Ted's hand and backed away until she was against the wall. Ted realised what she was looking at and tried to reassure her, "It's okay - this is my friend. I haven't named him yet though. Wasn't sure whether that would be a retarded thing to do, you know? Maybe you could think of a name for him?" He took a step forward and perched himself on the side of the bed. Nicola didn't move from where she was rooted to the spot.

"You need to go." Nicola said in a quiet voice.

"Need to go? I just fucking..." Ted corrected himself, "I'm sorry - I just got here. I just risked my life getting into the house so I could save you. I figured you'd be happy - what with all of your screaming."

"I was trying to get them away from my dad," Nicola said. She pointed out of the window towards the other house."

Ted followed her finger and saw what must have been her father in the house opposite.

"Well what's he doing over there?" he asked. Nicola made a sudden dash towards the door but Ted leaned forward and blocked her way with his arm. Before she could get away her pulled her close to his body. "You're a feisty little thing, aren't you?" She continued to struggle in his grip but he refused to let go, even with her crying out. "How old are you?" Ted asked. Nicola didn't answer. "Come on now, don't be shy. How old are you?" Ted repeated the question, his tone no longer the friendly tone he had initially approached her with.

"Seven..."

"Look I'm not going to hurt you. I'm just going to wait with you for a while, you know, to make sure your daddy gets home safely. I mean there's a lot of rotting dead fucks out there and he might be a little while...He'd want me to look after you." He paused. Nicola stopped struggling. "Okay? Does that sound fair to you? Surely it is better than being alone? Yeah?" He slowly released Nicola from his grip. As soon as he did so - she dove to the other side of the room, against the wall, again. Ted stood up and walked to the door. He closed it and turned to the window. He could see the young girl's father, across the road, at the doorway of the house. He opened it long enough to see it wasn't a viable option to escape from, considering the amount of infected headed his way. He slammed the door shut. "He might be a while," Ted said. He turned to Nicola. "Probably long enough

141

for you to thank me for helping you out," he said. He put the machete on the floor and slowly walked over to Nicola whilst undoing the belt on his trousers, "Damned thing," he said, "got covered in blood out there. No wonder you're scared of me - I probably look a right state." He kicked his trousers off and moved forward until he was standing uncomfortably close to Nicola. His penis was inches from her face and standing fully to attention. She turned away from him. "Have you ever seen one of these?" he asked. "No - of course not. Silly question." He paused. "Ever tasted one?"

## Michael

I slammed the front door shut. Fuck! Fuck! FUCK! The back door. I hurried through to the back door and yanked it open. I haven't found the keys yet and - quite frankly - I don't care. Can try and find them later when I know she is safe. For now I just need to get back to the house as quickly as possible. I jumped from the house, into the garden, and immediately attracted the attention of some of the infected milling around. Not enough room to get by them. Guess I'm going through them. I gripped the handle of the knife tightly.

## Dr. Platts

Every road I turned down was a similar story to the last.
Infected people standing around - as though they're waiting
for something to spark them into whatever form of life you'd
call this. Every time I came across another group, I'd turn
back the way I had come to try and find another route. I'm
not a strong person (physically) by any stretch of the
imagination. The last thing I'd want to do is try and fight any
of them - even with the clumsy slow speed they move at. I
backed up and turned back the way I had come. I'd only
parked my car a few streets from where I worked - where
there were no restrictions - and yet I just couldn't get to it. At
least not the ways I had tried. Just a few other alleyways and
roads I could try. I ran to the next junction and hung a right.
So tired and my ankle is killing me from the fall - at least I
presumed it was from the fall - but I couldn't stop moving.
Thankfully first impression of this road is that it is clear. A
promising start, I thought, as I started to run down it. Not the
quickest of routes but I should still be able to get to the car
from this road. As long as I could get to it - that'll do me.
Should have told Amy to meet me there but I figured, by the
time I explained what the car was and where it was parked,
we'd have run out of time anyway. It was the best thing to
do - to send her onto the supermarket via whichever route
she could find. As I continued to run down the empty road, I

couldn't help but wonder how she was getting on. Did she get there? Did she find a safe route? For her sake I hope so. Not just for her sake. I guess it would be nice to have some company in the supermarket, whilst we wait for the help to get to us.

"Hey! Over here! Are you bitten?" a voice called out. I turned in the direction of the sound. A young looking family were standing in the doorway of what must have been their home. The father was looking directly at me whilst the mother (at least I guessed she was the mother) was keeping an eye out for any potential trouble. "Are you bitten?" he asked again. I noticed the shovel in his hand. I guessed this was for protection and not for the intended use of digging.

"I'm not!"

"Come in! There's a few of us in here. You're welcome to wait..." A kind offer from a stranger. Maybe he felt he could trust me because of the way I was dressed and the fact I had a lanyard around my neck - suggesting I was a professional. Maybe he offered this to everyone. I don't know but it was unexpected. Part of me wanted to go with them. Part of me. The other part of me remembered how I came to be in the position I was in now and how very quickly the previous group had melted down. What was to stop the same happening with this new group? "Quickly!" he stepped to the side - allowing me to see into the house. I could see more people in the hallway. A few more appeared to be in what looked to be like the kitchen. I shook my head. "It's a good group," he shouted, "you're not safe out there."

"We're not safe anywhere," I pointed out. I turned away from him and continued my way down the road, in the vague direction of where I'd parked. The man didn't call out for me again. Instead I heard the sound of a front door slamming shut behind me. I should have told them I was going to the supermarket. I should have told them to come with me. Not sure how many people were in that house but they'll need food. They'll run out of food. Should go back and tell them of my plan. Tell them about Amy - and that she is on the way there now too. No. I can't go back. And we'd probably be safer in a smaller group. Less egos. Less opinions. Less chance of someone getting bitten and infecting the others if we stumbled across any potential trouble. At the end of the road and the next part of the route looks pretty much clear too with the exception of the odd infected. I still can't believe how quickly this took hold. One minute everything was normal, people were going about their lives and the next - the city is practically wiped out. I dread to think how many people have actually died now. I won't be one of them. I won't. I'll make it through this. I'll get to the supermarket, it will be clear and I'll hole up there until someone comes for me. And Amy will be there too. We'll both survive it. I ran down the side of the road with the least resistance and was soon standing at the mouth of the alleyway which would lead me to my car. I was apprehensive about venturing down it. It was tight with no way out if I were to run into trouble. Worst case scenario something would appear at the other end and I'd find myself blocked in by one of the infected in this street. I turned to look at them - they were slowly but surely making their way towards me. No doubt they were reacting to my heavy footsteps or breathing as I ran down the road. A quick check back down the alleyway - it's still clear. I have to go for it. Nothing certain about the next route being clear from danger if I don't go opt for this one. Okay. Can't stand here forever whilst trying to make my mind up. Just need to go for it. I set off down the alleyway being as quiet as I possibly good - yet maintaining a sensible speed. As I approached the other side, I slowed my pace to more of a crawl. Practically on tip-toes now as I listened out for the sounds of the dead. Can't hear anything. Has to be a good thing? Slowly I leaned out from the alleyway. There's a few of the dead further down the street but that's it. Seems to be pretty clear. I breathed a sigh of relief. My car was halfway down the street with nothing between us but space and litter. I couldn't have asked for a better outcome. I set off for the car with quickened steps, fishing in my pocket for the keys as I did so.

By the time I reached my car I had the car-key primed to slide it into the lock. Kind of wish I had one of the fobs which meant I could unlock the car from a distance but it's not the end of the world. They've heard me running for my car - the undead - but they're not close enough to pose me any threats. I slid the key into the lock and opened the door. Seconds later and the door was shut, the key in the ignition and my seat-belt securely fastened. I fired the engine up and pressed my foot down on the pedal. For the first time since everything kicked off, for the first time, I felt as though I had a genuine chance of surviving it.

I leaned across to the radio and pressed the 'on' switch. Nothing. Dead air. Damn. I was hoping for some kind of government issued message. Something to tell us - the survivors - where to go. Something to tell us that help was on the way. Dead air. An eerie silence. Not a good sign. Stick with the original plan. Head for the supermarket and see if Amy is there. The good news is - at this rate - I'll get there before the sun comes down. Daylight is another important factor between life and death.

## Michael

I ran across the street unarmed but I didn't care. I had lost the damned knife in the side of one of the infected head's I had stuck it into. Fucking thing snapped after I'd stuck it into the fourth, or fifth, forehead. No time to fret about the lack of weapon though. I looked up to the window as I crossed the street in the hope of seeing Nicola standing there - waving at me but she wasn't there. Only the curtain was a sign of life; gently flapping in the afternoon's breeze. Too many infected at the front door because she'd called them over. I had to run down the side of the house to check the back door. I was shocked at the sight of the back garden - a pile of dead bodies lying in various states of decay. My heart skipped a beat when I realised the back door was wide open. No. No. No. I ran in and slammed it shut behind me.

"Nicola!" I called out. "Honey!" No one answered my call. Not the sound of my daughter nor the sound of a stranger. "Anyone?" I called. A thud from upstairs. Someone still up there. Please be okay. Please be okay. I ran up the stairs and down the hallway towards the bedroom I'd last seen Nicola in. I got to the doorway and froze. A sinking feeling in the pit of my stomach. Standing in front of me was my baby girl. Her clothes on the floor in a messy heap, her once beautiful eyes now clouded over with death's curtain, her mouth gnashing and biting at thin air. She turned to me and cranked her head to the side. I dropped to my knees with tears streaming from my eyes as I noticed a gash in her stomach. A trickle of blood down the inside of her bare leg. "Oh no no no..." I shook my head as my mind ran through the horrors she'd been exposed to. In my mind they could have been worse than what she was actually forced to endure but I'd never know. Not for sure. I'd have to live with the knowledge that I'd failed her.

She started to move across the room towards me with her fingers outstretched to take  hold of me. Her head twitching and her mouth still biting at nothing. I held out my arms. I don't care anymore. Not for this, not for anything. I just want to be with my family and there's only one way I'll be able to do that now. There's only one way I'll find any peace. As my daughter neared, I pulled her close and held her to my body. I was quivering with fear as I felt her teeth sink into my neck. I wept as I knew it wouldn't be long before I joined her. I closed my eyes as she continued to bite and scratch me. The pain didn't bother me - not knowing the peace that was waiting for me on the other side. I opened my eyes as I felt a burning sensation tear through my body. There, over my daughter's shoulder, was my wife. She was smiling and beckoning me towards her - and the light shining brightly behind her. I felt my eyes slowly close. Feel. Heavy.

By the time I opened my eyes the pain had stopped. Not just that but I couldn't feel anything. I was standing next to my wife who was staring at me, smiling. I smiled at her.

"I've missed you," she said.

I wanted to tell her that I'd missed her too but I couldn't. I just broke down into tears. The sound of chewing from behind me. I turned around and saw my daughter hunched over my body on the other side of the room. Her hands wrapped around my face as she continued to bite into the top of my head - brains exposed, brains being chewed.

"I'm sorry," I told my wife, turning away from the horrors in front of us, "I couldn't protect her. I did what I could..."

Vix smiled, "No one could have protected her. It's too late for everyone. They just don't know it yet."

"But look at what's left of her..."

I wasn't sure why I hadn't turned into what my daughter had changed into. Maybe because she'd bitten into my brain? Maybe that was enough to stop me.

Vix reassured me, "That's not your daughter. Just as that's not you..." she nodded towards the violence behind me. I turned around and noticed that my body was sitting up; the same look on its face as that of my daughter's. "Come with me," Vix whispered, "Come be with your daughter and I." She took my hand and led me towards the light. I feel something. I feel warmth.

## Ted

I staggered through yet another alleyway on another god forsaken housing estate. These places are like a fucking maze. My mood somewhat dampened by the little fucker I'd earlier encountered. I hadn't been going to hurt her. I especially hadn't been going to kill her. All she had had to do was give me the necessary thanks for coming to her rescue. Didn't see the teeth coming. Credit where it was due, she was stronger than I first believed her to be. The only thing which didn't surprise me about that encounter was my temper. Soon as I felt the teeth against the shaft of my penis, I felt the blinding rage erupting from within. I grabbed her by the scruff of her neck, pulled her away and threw her against the wall like a little rag-doll. Looking back, now I've had a chance to calm down a little, I feel as though I may have been a little over the top with regards to my reaction. Should have just fucked her. That would have been punishment enough. Shouldn't have stuck her with Bob The Machete. Is that guilt? What a strange emotion. Stranger now to sense it when the world has gone fuck up. Put that shit out of my mind. Wipe that crap away. New World, New Rules. Fuck it. What's done is done. No sense crying over spilt milk. Although it will be a different story if I start to turn into one of the rotting dead fucks - a thought which has been plaguing me ever since the little cunt put tooth to cock. I tried to put it from my mind as I finally found a main road. Not sure how but I'm no longer on the housing estate. I'm back on the road where I had watched the truck hit the girl....And speaking of the truck. I can see it now. It's heading for me. The front of it is bashed beyond recognition. How the thing is still driving is beyond me. I put my hands up in the air and waved towards the driver - less chance of the same happening to me as happened to the woman considering the truck's pretty much cleared the area of R.D.Fs thanks to it's previous erratic driving. Even so, I prepared myself to dive from the path.

I expected the truck to speed up and try and hit me. At the very least I expected it to go round me. If it were me in there, I wouldn't be stopping for anything. Not that stupid. To my surprise the vehicle slowed. I heard the doors lock before the window opened as it pulled up to my side. I looked in - a black man at the wheel with a maniacal grin on his face. Fuck his teeth are white. Wouldn't want to hide down a dark alleyway with him unless he could promise not to grin.

"You bit?" he asked. I have to confess - at first - I didn't have a fucking clue what he was saying. His accent was that thick. When my brain figured it out I managed to answer him a 'no'. Thought he probably didn't need to know about the girl. Not as though she was one of the dead fucks anyway. "Where you headed?" he asked. Again - a few seconds to figure out what actually came from his mouth. I shrugged. "I need petrol," he said. Honestly it was like watching a foreign film minus the subtitles. I couldn't help but wonder whether this was how deaf people felt when they tried understanding someone who was a little quieter than others. "You help me

152

out, I give you a lift." Seemed like a fair deal when my brain processed the words. I shouldn't grumble. At least he spoke my language. "You def not bit?" he repeated.

"No."

I heard the door unlock. He leaned across and opened the passenger door. I took that as all the invitation I needed and went and climbed in, closing the door behind me.

"So where's the nearest petrol station?" he asked. I thought, for a minute, and could only think of one; the supermarket. I directed him as best as I could and we set upon our path - hitting anything which walked with satisfying thuds.

"What's your name?" I asked.

"Abrafo," he said. It was no good, I had to ask him to repeat it three times.

"What? Your mum and dad must have fucking hated you. You bullied a lot at school?" he looked at me with piercing black eyes.

"It comes from a military term. It means executioner," he informed me. Oh - well excuse me all to hell. Apt meaning though - considering what he had done to the woman.

"Well - I think if it's all the same with you - I'm going to call you Colin." The man gave me another stern look. Don't give a fuck. I'm the one with Bob the machete. He wants to try anything, I'll just fuck him up. I didn't see why he should be offended. It's not as though people like him don't rename themselves all the time. Only the other week - before things turned to shit - I had a phone call from some foreign fuck overseas trying to sell me a mobile phone. The first thing which annoyed me about the phone call was the fact that he tried to sell me a mobile phone by phoning my mobile phone.

"Do you currently have a mobile phone?" he'd asked. He knew the fucking answer. He'd called me on it! The second thing which annoyed me was the fact he introduced himself as John. No way was he a John. Not a fucking chance. And if he was able to lie about his name - what else was the cunt able to lie about?

My mind switched back to seeing Colin run the girl over earlier and I couldn't help but to bring it up. My mind curious as to what was going through his head, "So - what - you just going round running everyone over?" I asked. Was I only safe because he needed directions to the petrol station? What with him clearly not being from the area.

"I kill the dead," he told me. His voice was so serious about it. Like a man on a mission. I quite like that.

"What about the girl?"

"What girl?"

I explained to him that I'd witnessed him plough into a girl who was trying to get his attention and I stifled a laugh when I saw the look of horror on his face. He hadn't realised he'd seen anyone else alive - other than me - and had just been trying to send as many of the R.D.Fs back to Hell as he possibly could. That's fucking priceless.

"I thought you of all people would have stopped for her," I continued. "Taken her home...I mean - that's what your kind does with pretty white girls, isn't it? They just take 'em home and make them their bitch - or they rape them..."

The man slammed on the brakes and we skidded to a halt. "Get the fuck out!" he yelled at me. "Racist piece of shit." I had to ask him to repeat the last sentence twice. An R.D.F starting banging on the window of my side of the truck. He yelled at me (which didn't help his accent), "GET THE FUCK OUT!" I raised Bob to the man's throat.

"Let's not be too hasty, shall we? I'll cut you. Now. You need me and I fancy a lift anyway. The supermarket will serve us both. I'll help you get petrol and then I'll go off my own way..." my own way being the supermarket. Fucking starving. Only had had a few bars of chocolate and that isn't enough to keep me going. Colin, for that was his name, raised his hands as though on the defensive. Can't say I blame him - pretty sure I'd have done the same thing if someone had aimed Bob at my throat. "Good. Glad you understand." I pulled the blade away but kept it primed to take a swing if need be. "Drive on, Jeeves." I could tell that Colin hated me. I could see it in his eyes that he wanted the R.D.F to pull me through the window but I didn't give a fuck. I'm smarter than this ape. Always have been and always will be. Colin pressed down on the gas and we moved on - with the truck stuttering in the process. "You sure you have enough petrol to even get us there?" I asked.

## Dr. Platts

I drove all the way up to the supermarket - right up to the main entrance. I'd already realised this wasn't the plan I had hoped it would be. The infected were in the car park, freely roaming, and - when I stopped by the entrance - the automatic doors were working as though powered by a generator. Good that there was power but not good that the doors worked as it meant anything could wander in without too much trouble. Well I need to have a look at least. Need to see if Amy is there. Just stick my head in, have a quick scan of the place and - if there is trouble - get the Hell out of there. Maybe be able to grab some of the food from the shelves before making my retreat? No sense second guessing what will happen or what I'll be able to do. Just need to get in there and see what is what. I took a few deep breaths to steady my nerves. Really wish I had someone with me for a little moral support right about now. Being alone - in a time like this - is no fun at all. Okay. This is it. I took the key from the ignition and opened the car door. I didn't bother locking the door as I entered the supermarket. I wanted it to be easy to just open and door and jump in - just in case I am chased out by something, or someone.

Inside the supermarket was a mess. Clearly people had been having the same plans as us. Shelves had clearly been ransacked - some had toppled over. There were broken food packages on the floor with clear signs they'd been trampled on. A few bodies which had been torn to pieces. They weren't showing signs of infection but - even so - I kept my distance from them. I hadn't gone far into the supermarket but I already knew Amy wasn't in here. She wouldn't have stayed in here. I know because I won't stay in here. It's not the safe haven I had hoped it to be. That much is clear. I grabbed a basket from the floor and hurried to the first aisle - just grab enough food to see me through the next few days. Maybe head out to the country and see if there are any retreats out there? I knew of a rehab centre on the outskirts of town - those things are so secure and fussy about who comes and goes that there was a good chance it would be....A noise distracted me; a jar broke on the floor somewhere. Don't waste time thinking; just grab what I can and get out of here. It's not safe. The first aisle had fruit and vegetables. Not the best of food to take due to their limited shelf life but it didn't matter. As long as it lasted a couple of days that would be fine. They'll be good for that. I grabbed what I could and threw it into the basket whilst keeping an eye out all around for any signs of the infected. I know they're in here. Jars don't just topple onto the floor without something to push them.

With the basket full I turned back to the entrance point of the store. The automatic doors slid open before I got there and I froze on the spot. Was someone out there? Was someone coming in? I know I received some attention as I drove into the building but I didn't see any of the infected being close enough to get there so quickly. Not with the speed they move. Another smash from behind me made me spin on the spot. Still can't see any signs of life (or infected) from behind me even though I know something is back there. It doesn't matter - not going that way. Need to go through the front door. Need to get back to my car. Just make a run for it. I only need to make it to the car - which is open - and then I'm safe. I can do it...Okay. A took a few deep breaths. Any hesitation I was to potentially suffer disappeared at the sound of another breaking jar from somewhere behind me. I ran for the door. As I neared, the automatic door slid open allowing my freedom. I can see the car. I can see the sky. I can see the floor. I can see my body. I can see the floor. I can see an infected in the distance. I can see two figures next to my body. I can see the sky. I can see the floor. I head-butted the floor. I rolled to the side. Concrete. Sky. Concrete. Sky. Concrete. Sky. Concrete. Sky. Concrete. Sky. Two figures next to my body; one cheering, one screaming. I came to a rest as my eye-sight faded. Hearing was the last thing to go. The sound of cheering.

## Ted

I stopped cheering when I saw the horror on Colin's face. "That's one all," I reminded him. "I thought she was one of the rotting dead fucks!" I lied. I saw through the window who it was. All my Christmases had come at once too. Always wanted to cut her head off. And the fucking way it flew from her shoulders - well that was my main Christmas present right there. I continued, "You're going to need a stronger stomach if you're to survive in this world, my friend. Can't always hide behind a steering wheel to do your killing. Survival of the sickest. Remember that - it'll serve you well." I wiped the Bob clean on my trousers and stepped through the sliding doors and into the store. Colin followed.

We'd made it to the petrol station but couldn't get the damned pumps to work. I thought it was a matter of just squeezing the trigger as usual but apparently not. There was no chance we were going to make it to the next station so I told Colin I was going to the supermarket to get some food and see if anyone else was around. Of all the people to run into. Dr-fucking-Platts. Still laughing now. Such a great fucking shot with the machete. Man - had I known the end of the world was going to be this fun - I'd have wished for it a lot sooner. Not that I actually wished for it. Sure I wished I was dead from time to time but not now. Now I'm glad I never had the balls to kill myself. I'd have missed out on this; the chance to live out all the fantasies society tends to frown upon. Anyway, Colin had come with me because he didn't fancy going it alone and I didn't mind. Figured - with the lights out - he'd be good for the odd sneak attack. As long as he squinted - what with the whites of his eyes being as bright as his smile.

"Should start at the tool section," I told him, "see if we can find you a weapon." I scanned the signs above the many aisles hoping to see one which would point us in the direction of the tools. Instead something else caught my eye. "This way," I ordered him. Truth be told - he didn't have to follow and I wouldn't have given a fuck either way. He still followed. The way he took my order; they make good fucking slaves. No wonder we shipped them overseas to help us out. We hurried towards the aisle which had caught my attention - clothes.

"What are you doing?" he asked (at least I think that's what he said) as I started thumbing my way through the trainers which hung from the rack. He was looking around nervously.

"Have you seen my shoes?" I asked him. They were on their way out long before all of this kicked off but - yeah - the last two days had seriously taken their toll, what with all the running and walking. And the toe-punt to the zombie's head back in the garden - that didn't help. I mean - fuck - every time I go through a puddle of gore I get wet socks. You know how irritating that is? I found a pair of trainers which looked as though they were ripped off directly from a pair of Nikes.

They'd do. I pulled them off the shelf where they hung by a small hanger and kicked my own shoes off.

"We need to get out of here!" Colin said. His voice was panicked. "Can you hear them?" He wasn't hearing things. I could definitely hear the groans of trouble but I also knew they were distant enough not to cause us any issues. Not yet anyway. I slid the new trainers on.

"Oh my God - so fucking soft!" I stood up and did a couple of test jumps. "You not going to get yourself a new pair whilst we're here?" He didn't answer. He was staring dead ahead at something behind me. Two of the R.D.Fs were approaching us.

"We need to go!" he shouted again. He turned and ran in the opposite direction. I didn't have to follow him. It was only two. I could have taken them down. Didn't though. I followed like a little sheep. Having him around - he was a good look-out if nothing else. I could have sworn those fuckers were further away from me.

"Where the fuck are you going?" I shouted at him as he led the way through the back of the store. "We could have just gone out via the front!" We were running through the back area with no idea of where we were headed. Colin clearly running in a blind panic - completely lost. As he turned another corner he spotted another room to charge into. He opened the door and burst in without a care for what he was running into. Only caring about what he was running away from. "Just stop a minute!" I called out. "We need to think this through..." We'd run so far and fast that there was no

chance we were still being chased. Once in the room Colin
ran to the next door and gave the handle a try. It was locked.
"Brilliant! Now won't you just fucking calm down a minute
and let us think this through sensibly?" I was glad he had
cornered us - gave me a minute to catch my breath. Little
fucker certainly could run. Guess they have to over there
though.

"Look!" they'd call out to each other, "Clean water!" and
they'd run towards it before the others lapped it all up.
That's how it is in my head anyway and I doubt I'm wrong.
No other reason they're all Speedy-Gonzales.

"Fuck!" Colin hit the locked door and turned back to me. He
froze on the spot. I did too - something about the look on his
face. A groan from close behind me. I span around and
realised we'd burst straight into a room and past one of the
rotting dead fucks. A female security officer. Mid thirties,
white shirt, short black dress - kind of hot if I'm going to be
honest. I jumped back and got behind the desk in the middle
of the room. "She's blocking our way out!" Colin observed.
Well done Colin. Good observational skills. I noticed a
bloodied knife on the desk and grabbed it. I handed it to
Colin. "What is this for?"

"Think about it, you fucking idiot!" The woman had a slit
across her neck. I wondered whether she'd taken her own
life - knowing she was doomed anyway - or whether
someone else had taken it from her. I wouldn't have. Far too
pretty to kill. She wasn't moving towards us, just standing
there in front of the door, snarling with a look of hunger in

her eyes. "We can rush her," I told him. "You step out that way," I pointed him in the direction I needed him to go, "and I'll go in the other way. Whichever one of us that she doesn't look towards needs to run forward to stab her in the head. Get it? Quite a fucking simple plan!"

"I don't know if I can."

"Of course you can, you've been killing them all morning!"

"In my car!"

"Okay - step out and distract her and I'll charge towards her!" He hesitated for a moment until he realised that - if he didn't want to kill her - it was his best option. He stepped from behind the desk and took a step towards her, ready to turn and run if she suddenly lunged. Silly though - he shouldn't have turned away from me. I was more of a danger than one of the Rotting Dead Fucks. I lunged forward from behind the desk and swiped at the back of his leg with the machete. He screamed as a stream of blood flew towards the R.D.F which seemed to come alive at the scent of it. "Sorry, Colin, but - you know - I needed a distraction...Can't get more distracting than a screaming black man!" I hurried towards the door he'd previously said was locked. Hadn't tried it myself. Maybe it was just jammed. A twist of the handle. Definitely locked - fuck it. I turned back to the door. The R.D.F was greedily eating at Colin who was still screaming. Her hands ripping into his guts. All red on the inside. Guess - beneath the layers - we are the same. There's a lesson there not that I'll bother to learn it. I made a move for the door but the R.D.F suddenly turned to face me. I backed up behind the desk again and she continued to eat Colin. There's not enough room to make a run for it. Not sure I'd get past without her grabbing me. I sunk down behind the desk while I weighed up my options.

Present Day

\* \* \*

There is no escape from it

His name was Ted

"Just think of it as lubrication," she said. She rubbed her clitoris with one hand (in my mind) and took a hold of my penis with her other hand (again, in my mind). She didn't hesitate in guiding me in. Damn soft. Wet. Surprisingly warm despite the look of her suggesting she'd been dead for more than a few days. Fuck. They should bottle this shit and sell it via online sex shops. That is, after they've figured out how to get the Internet back online again. Priorities and all that. "How is it?" she purred.

"Fucking good." I couldn't contain my excitement as I started to build into a steady rhythm. To think, after I had killed her, I had collapsed from tiredness. Must be having my second wind. "What about you?" I asked her. "Good?"

"The best," she smiled at me with her dead face. I looked down at my cock as it pushed in and pulled out of her sopping cunt. Strings of black tar clinging to it. In my mind it wasn't black tar or anything as sick. In my mind it was her juicy cunt batter sticking to my cock. I couldn't contain myself and withdrew quickly before I moved down her body

167

until I was mouth to pussy. My brain was screaming 'no' somewhere inside but my body (my tongue in particular) chose to ignore it and I found myself greedily lapping at her sour milk despite a gagging reflex. Don't care. So fucking horny and so...I stopped. My tongue was numb. Numb, that is, other than a strange tingling sensation as though it were trying to wake up. A burning feeling scalding the back of my throat. Eyes and nose streaming. What the fuck is this?

"What have you fucking done to me?" I asked the dead girl. She did not respond. With her eyes at the back of her head still - she wasn't even looking at me. Colin was, though. He was looking right at me. A look of satisfaction on his face. A look of justice. I staggered back against the wall and pulled myself up. "What have you fucking done?" I screamed again. The words didn't sound quite right though. I dropped to my knees as my legs gave way; the same numb feeling killing my tongue. "What glerk ark hack," weren't the words I was trying to spit. Panic rushed through me. At least I think it did - everything is numb. My arms and legs flailing all over the place as I struggle to maintain control over my body.

Colin fucking laughing at me. His dead eyes fixed upon me. I'm sure I heard him say, "You did this to yourself." I fell forward onto my face. It should have hurt but the numbness meant I felt nothing. I was grateful for that at....brains. Warm tasty brains. Brains. Brains.
Braiiiiiiiiiiinnnnnsssssssssss................

THE END

Rotting Dead F*cks

Want to follow the work of Matt Shaw?

The published author of over fifty books - all readily available on Amazon - Matt Shaw can be found on his Facebook Page

http://www.facebook.com/mattshawpublications.co.uk

Printed in Great Britain
by Amazon

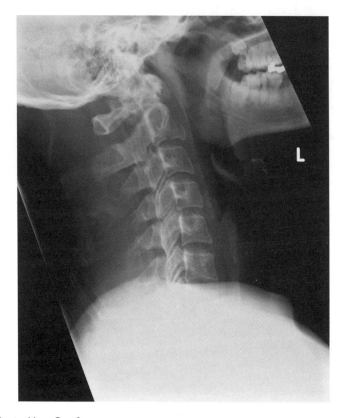